Arranged Marriages in India

A CASE FOR REVIEW

MANISH DIWADKAR

INDIA • SINGAPORE • MALAYSIA

ISBN 979-8-89446-329-2

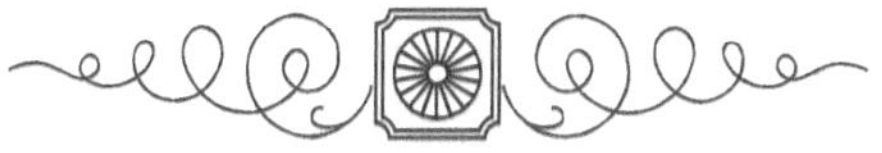

Acknowledgements

I need to acknowledge the efforts of those who have helped me with my maiden book. Firstly, I thank my Associate Advocate Tejaswi More who not only persuaded me to write this book but also helped me with typing of the original handwritten manuscript.

Secondly, I thank my Associate Advocate Pooja Rane who helped me with the proof reading of the entire manuscript.

And, last but not the least, I thank my publishers Notion Press Media Pvt. Ltd., and their entire editorial and publishing team. I especially thank Rohan Reddy, Publishing Consultant, for explaining to me the entire publishing process and helping me select the appropriate publishing plan, and Neha Thomas, Publishing Manager, for guiding me through every stage of the publication process and helping my maiden book see the light of day.

Mumbai,
25th June, 2024 — Manish Diwadkar

To My Beloved Wife

LATIKA

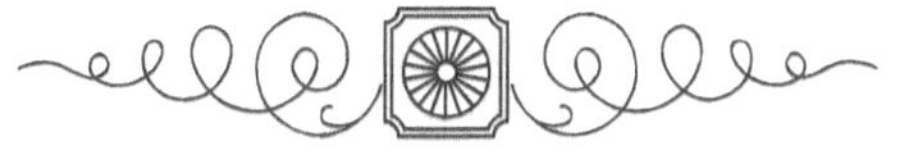

I

CIRCA: 2005. Vikrant had flown down to Mumbai for a month. This time, his visit had a definite purpose—marriage. No, please don't jump to any conclusions. Vikrant's marriage had not yet been fixed. It was only under contemplation, but he was expected to get married during this visit. In case you are wondering how this was possible within a span of a month, the 'bride-searching' process had already commenced a couple of months prior to Vikrant's visit. His mother used to email him the photographs and other particulars about prospective brides, and Vikrant would short-list a few of them. Actually, the process worked the other way around; Vikrant would 'reject' some of the proposals, and what remained would, therefore, qualify as having been short-listed.

Now, firstly, can there be anything such as 'bride-searching'? It is as if you go all over town looking for prospective brides. Just imagine popping the question to a good-looking girl, who would appear to be a prospective bride at a mall, a railway station, or on a bus. Thankfully, things have not become so awful yet. Then, how exactly does this process of 'bride-searching' work? Well, you have professional marriage bureaus that stack up data on prospective brides and grooms, and fix up matches as per particular requirements. Then, there are newspaper columns that run matrimonial advertisements, where you can invite offers from prospective brides and grooms based on your specified requirements. Doesn't all this sound more like a 'used-car-for-sale' advertisement? Finally, there are the aunts who do 'marriage-fixing' more as a 'hobby' rather than a business. In Vikrant's case, it was an aunt who was playing the role of 'facilitator'.

When Vikrant actually landed in Mumbai, he had four girls lined up for him. No, Vikrant was not going to have any *Swayamvar* or anything of that sort. What he was going to do was to have a 'girl-seeing programme'. What exactly is that? Well, you see, Vikrant, accompanied by his parents and, maybe, his 'facilitator' aunt and a couple of cousins, who want to be part of the '*ladkewale*', will visit the prospective bride's residence to 'see' her. The prospective bride would be accompanied by her '*ladkiwale*', which would include her parents, siblings, uncle and aunt or, in some cases, even neighbours. At these 'girl-seeing-programmes' the '*ladkewales*' 'see' the girl as if she is some exhibit on display for prospective purchasers. The girl, i.e., the prospective bride, has to face a barrage of questions from the 'ladkewales', and if she is equal to the task and is able to meet their requirements, then the '*ladkewales*' leave after dropping a hint that the proposal is under positive consideration. If the girl i.e. the prospective bride fails the test, then the '*ladkewales*' leave after simply saying, "We'll let you know". Often, the expression conveys the underlying decision. The point to be noted here is that it's always the boy's prerogative to select or reject the girl as if the girl has no feelings, emotions, choices, or rights. The entire process of rejection is so demeaning to the girl as if she is some exhibit for sale.

Now, coming back to the four short-listed girls by Vikrant. Since the photographs of the girls had played a crucial role in the short-listing process; you can safely assume that all the four girls were good-looking—read 'fair'. In India, when any girl is referred to as 'good-looking' or 'beautiful', you can safely presume that the girl is fair. The Indians' obsession with fairness goes back to the British era when they were over-awed by the 'beauty' of the '*gorimemsaabs*'. Not for nothing do fairness creams do brisk business in India. Apart from the 'looks' aspect, the other factor that was considered during the short-listing process was the 'family background'. Now, that would mean and include the professional background of the girl's father, grandfather, mother, uncles and aunts. If the girl's great-grandfather had been awarded 'Rai Bahadur' during the pre-Independence era, it would qualify as a very good 'family background'. Or, that the girl's great-grandfather owned a 'Plymouth' or a 'Morris' during 'those days' would qualify her family as being '*Khandaani*'. How such a family background can help in the success of a marriage in the 21st century is difficult to fathom. Be that as it may, Vikrant had short-listed four girls, viz. Nisha, Rhea, Mohini, and Shweta. Wow!! It almost feels as if these four girls have been short-listed for the final round of the Miss World pageant. Isn't that great? Every Indian girl who has an 'arranged marriage' can experience the euphoria of being selected for the final round of a beauty pageant at some stage in her life.

The first girl Vikrant 'saw' was Nisha. The advantage for the girl who is 'seen' first is that the '*ladkewales*' don't come with the baggage of past experiences. So, the first girl is normally 'screened' without any preconceived thoughts and ideas. Nisha came across as a very confident, aggressive, and dynamic girl. She knew what she wanted out of life. She was a management graduate who was employed with a financial institution. As one eager to climb the corporate ladder, she could give any man worth his degree a run for his job. Now, this was not a healthy sign; in the long run, she could severely dent Vikrant's male ego if she were to be more successful than him in their respective careers. In India, the husband is always supposed to earn more than his wife. The role of the working wife is only to earn that much, which would help in reducing the monthly EMIs of a housing loan. She is not supposed to think of career advancement or better job prospects so as to surpass her husband in earning potential or income levels. So, Nisha's confidence, aggressiveness, and dynamism proved her undoing. She was 'rejected' by Vikrant.

The next girl Vikrant 'saw' was Rhea. She was a vivacious and bubbly girl. Rhea was a creative person employed with an advertising agency. The only redeeming feature about these 'girl-seeing-programmes' is that they allow the boy and girl to spend about 15-20 minutes by themselves, whereby they can get to know each other better. How one can take a life-changing decision within 15-20 minutes beats me. Even job interviews last longer, and there, both parties have the option of correcting a wrong choice made without much damage, monetary or otherwise. So, at this particular session, Vikrant got to spend a few minutes with Rhea. During the conversation, it emerged that Rhea had had a boyfriend with whom she had broken off about a year ago. Whether Vikrant was immodest or brave, or both, he did enquire whether Rhea had been intimate with her ex. Now, in India, there are many misconceptions about a girl's virginity. If the girl does not bleed during the first intercourse, it's presumed that she is not a virgin. Gynaecologists have gone on record to state that a girl can lose her virginity (in medical terminology, split her hymen) for reasons other than sexual intercourse. Another belief is that virginity is the best gift that a wife can present to her husband. But, hold on; why are we discussing virginity only vis-à-vis the wife? What about the virginity of the husband? Indian men either don't know that the concept of virginity applies to them as well, or they pretend not to know it, or worse still, they really believe that there is no such thing as male virginity. So, coming back to Vikrant's question, Rhea candidly admitted that she had had sex with her ex. Now, this admission on the part of Rhea amounted to blasphemy in an 'arranged marriage'. So, Rhea's candidness sealed her fate. She was 'rejected' by Vikrant.

The third girl Vikrant 'saw' was Mohini. She had an outgoing personality and was employed as a fashion designer with an Indian label. She was all-out to impress Vikrant because, through him, she wanted to realise her big American dream. Yes, Vikrant was a software engineer in the USA, and marrying him would give Mohini an opportunity to migrate to the Big Apple, where she could realise her dream of working for a big name in the fashion industry. And, eventually, maybe, it would be her passport to Paris, Milan, and London. Normally, during the 'girl-seeing programmes', the girl is dressed in traditional Indian wear. But Mohini, being a fashion designer with an American dream, was dressed in an outfit that made her look as if she was on a catwalk. Her animated conversation with Vikrant made him realise that Mohini was only using him as a ladder to pursue her own agenda. Mohini was physically present in India, but mentally, she was already living her American dream.

Now, Vikrant was not someone who would fall for the guile of Mohini. Needless to say, Mohini too was 'rejected' by Vikrant.

Vikrant was now getting sceptical about finding a bride. One week and three 'girl-seeing programmes' later, the question that stared him in the face was, if he had to return to America without a wife, he would not be able to fly down to Mumbai for at least a couple of years. That meant no marriage on the cards for the next two years at least. Maybe he should have short-listed a couple more girls; that would have perhaps brightened his chances of landing a bride. Vikrant had three more weeks in India and one more girl to 'see'. His mother again contacted the aunt who was playing the role of a 'facilitator'. The 'facilitator' aunt pacified Vikrant's mother. She assured Vikrant's mother that her network was wide enough and she would definitely manage to hunt down a bride for Vikrant within the next week. The whole process was suddenly sounding and feeling bizarre. It was as if Vikrant was looking out for a pet to carry back with him, and the pets on display in the pet-shop were not up to Vikrant's fancy, so the pet-shop owner had promised to hunt one down which would be to Vikrant's specifications. Hello!! We are not talking of a St. Bernard dog or a Siamese cat here. We are talking of a wife—a girl with feelings, emotions, ambitions, aspirations, ideas, views, opinions, plans and, above all, love. Assuming that the 'facilitator' aunt would actually manage to locate a prospective bride for Vikrant even within a week, don't Vikrant and the girl have to know each other well enough before tying the knot? In Vikrant's case, time was at a premium. Fine. But, what about love? Love? In arranged marriages in India, a marriage is performed first; love happens afterwards; or at least, love is supposed to follow the marriage. The bride and groom are expected to fall in love with each other after marriage. As if, they have a choice. And, what would happen if, in a given case, the couple does not fall in love with each other? Shh... Such questions are not asked in India. Arranged marriages are a time-tested tradition in India; nobody has ever questioned its intrinsic value. People have been getting married in this way through the ages, and nobody has ever complained with respect to the merits of the system. On the contrary, grandparents recite, with much humour, their stories of only having seen each other's photographs prior to their marriage. Then, why suddenly this scepticism about Vikrant's intended arranged marriage?

Vikrant was now gearing himself to 'see' Shweta. He was not really sure of what to expect. He had already experienced supreme confidence, pre-marital sex, and personal agendas in his previous encounters. He was wondering what surprises Shweta would throw at him.

Shweta was Vikrant's maternal aunt's sister-in-law's friend's neighbour's daughter. Understood the relation?

No? Neither did I, but this is how arranged marriages are fixed in India. By the way, Vikrant's maternal aunt's sister-in-law was the 'facilitator' aunt. Shweta was a postgraduate in English literature and was employed as a lecturer in a city college. Her father held a top managerial position with a financial institution; her mother was a housewife and her younger sister was studying to be a chartered accountant. Now, this would qualify as a good 'family background'. In Indian arranged marriages, family background plays a vital role, as an Indian arranged marriage is as much a marriage between the families of the bride and groom as it is between the bride and the groom. Shweta's family background was commensurate with that of Vikrant's. Vikrant's father was earlier employed with an MNC, but had quit to start his own business. Although Vikrant's father would have been happier if Vikrant had joined him in his business, Vikrant wanted to pursue his American dream. Maybe, at a later stage, he would return to India and join hands with his father in running the latter's business. Vikrant's mother was actively involved with an NGO for destitute children, which was more of a social responsibility rather than a means of income. Vikrant's younger sister was pursuing a course in business management.

Would Vikrant be fourth time lucky? Will Vikrant's search for a bride end at Shweta's doorstep? Will Vikrant finally manage to return to America with a wife in tow?

When Vikrant went to 'see' Shweta, he was accompanied by his parents, his maternal aunt, and his maternal cousin. The 'facilitator' aunt, along with her friend, was already present at Shweta's residence. After the formal introductions and initial exchange of pleasantries were over, Shweta's father gestured to her that she and Vikrant could move over to her bedroom for a private conversation. Accordingly, Shweta led Vikrant to her bedroom.

Shweta's bedroom was a cosy little room stacked with a lot of books. It was apparent that Shweta was a voracious reader. In the array of books on the bookshelf were Shakespeare's "The Complete Works"; a motley collection of Charles Dickens; "Pygmalion" by George Bernard Shaw; Emily Brontë's "Wuthering Heights"; so also, Jane Austen's "Pride and Prejudice" occupied a place of pride on the bookshelf. On the writing table lay a book that contained a collection of poems by William Wordsworth, with a bookmark peeping out from one of the pages. On the wall beside her bed hung a photograph of Shweta taken on the occasion of her convocation. The ocular impression that Shweta's bedroom conveyed was unmistakable viz. that its occupant was academically inclined.

Vikrant was immediately struck by the contrast of Shweta's bedroom vis-à-vis his own. Vikrant's bedroom back home had a huge poster of a 'Kawasaki' sports bike hung on one of its walls. On another wall was pasted a life-size poster of Bruce Springsteen in a singing pose, strumming a guitar, blaring "Dancing in the Dark" into the microphone. In another corner on the wall were pasted posters of a bevvy of Hollywood beauties, including Jennifer Lopez, Salma Hayek, Penélope Cruz, Catherine Zeta-Jones, and Angelina Jolie. The first impression that Vikrant's bedroom would convey about him was that he was someone who did not take life too seriously; one who enjoyed the good things in life; one who lived life in the fast lane; generally, a 'cool' type of guy.

Shweta pulled out the chair tucked under the writing table and gestured for Vikrant to take a seat. Vikrant plonked himself into the chair, whilst simultaneously nodding a 'thank-you'. Shweta seated herself on her bed. It was Vikrant who broke the ice.

V: "You seem to be an avid reader."

S: "English literature is my passion, and now, also my profession."

V: "That's not my forte; I'd rather dabble in computers."

Shweta gave a half-smile.

V: "Aren't you on Facebook? I confess, I did try to search for you but didn't find you."

S: "I'm not much of a social person, whether online or off."

V: "And friends?"

S: "I have a few friends, mostly from the faculty. Otherwise, books are my constant companion."

V: "How do you spend your time, especially weekends?"

S: "We may go to the theatre, music concerts, or maybe for dinner."

V: "With family?"

S: "Mostly."

V: "In America, we work hard, and party even harder. I party with my friends on Friday and Saturday evenings. And, sometimes we have weekend getaways."

S: "Oh!"

V: "Don't you party with friends?"

S: "No. Not much."

After a pause.

S: "Don't feel the need to."

V: "Wow! You're the intelligent type, eh?"

S: "You, too, are intelligent. But, I suppose it's a matter of choice; of what makes you happy. Reading gives me pleasure; you may find it boring."

V: "Have you been to America before?"

S: "No. We have only been to Bangkok, Pattaya, and Singapore on a holiday."

V: "But, you wouldn't mind staying in America, would you? I mean, adjusting to the American way of life."

S: "I think life is all about making adjustments. And, life everywhere is not much different. After all, all over the world people work to earn their livelihood, they eat three meals a day; they all strive to make their life more comfortable. The only difference is in the availability of infrastructure, and, maybe, that would make a difference in the level of comfort."

V: "My God! What philosophy."

In the meantime, the guests seated outside were served with tea, coffee, and snacks. One of the items served was 'moong dal halwa', supposedly prepared by Shweta. The guests were being coaxed by Shweta's mother into having a second helping of the 'halwa'. In these 'girl-seeing programmes', the girl is always expected to serve a dish specially prepared by her for the occasion to display her culinary skills. This way, the '*ladkewales*' are assured that the girl knows cooking. Shweta's neighbouring aunt brought tea, coffee, and snacks for Shweta and Vikrant in the bedroom itself. She made it clear to Vikrant that the 'halwa' was prepared by Shweta especially for the occasion, lest he think that it was from a nearby 'halwai'. Vikrant put a morsel of the 'halwa' into his mouth.

V: "Hmm!! Superb!! You must be a very good cook?"

S: "Thanks to my mom; she taught me cooking when I was in school. My mom always used to tell me that, howsoever successful a woman becomes in her career, she has to cook for her family. You can say, it's my mom's '*Sanskaar*'."

V: "I can see it."

Vikrant finished the bowl of 'moong dal halwa' while simultaneously lavishing praise on Shweta's cooking abilities. Shweta felt flattered.

V: "You are a lecturer now, right? In case you have to migrate to America, what would you do there?"

S: "Well, I have given it a thought. Maybe, I can pursue my doctorate in English literature and try to join some university as faculty."

V: "Good planning, I must say."

S: "Thanks."

Just then, Shweta's mother peeped into the bedroom to see if the conversation was over so that the two of them could join the others outside in the drawing room. To Shweta's mother's enquiry, Vikrant unilaterally replied, "Yes, Aunty. We have had a good conversation. I don't think there are any more questions to be asked."

What Vikrant meant was that he did not have any more questions to ask. You see, these are 'girl-seeing-programmes', which essentially mean that the boy goes to 'see' the girl. So, it is the boy's prerogative to ask questions to the girl. The girl is only supposed to answer the questions posed by the boy. It is the boy who is going to 'see' the girl, meaning thereby, it is for the boy to either select or reject the girl. The girl has no say in the proceedings. If the boy says 'yes' to the girl, she is supposed to feel elated. And, in the 'unfortunate' event of being 'rejected' by the boy, the girl is expected to wallow in self-pity and attribute the 'rejection' to causes like being dark, overweight, too thin, too short, wearing glasses, not having long hair, not having a sweet voice, and what have you. The real merits of the girl are never taken into consideration; and, how do you expect the merits to be considered in a half-hour conversation?

And what if the girl wanted to ask certain questions to the boy? What if the girl wants to know whether the boy is a virgin? What if the girl wants to know the boy's income? What if the girl wants to know about the boy's drinking habit or whether he smokes? What if the girl wants to know about the boy's future plans? Don't even think about it, for the girl will immediately be labelled as over-confident, too smart, too outgoing and not homely enough or not wife material.

The general perception about these 'girl-seeing programmes' is that it is the girl who is in desperate need of getting married, and the boy is doing her a big favour by coming to 'see' her and an even greater favour if he actually says 'yes' to her. It was as if the girl was to die a spinster if the boy had not said 'yes' to her. On the contrary, it is the boys who are desperate to get married so that their burgeoning libidos can be satisfied without finding themselves in conflict with any legal statutes or on the wrong side of any moral values and social norms.

As Vikrant got up from the chair to leave the bedroom, Shweta blurted, "Excuse me!" Vikrant looked at her questioningly.

S: "I just wanted to know whether you had any plans of returning to India."

V: "Hmm. Well, at the moment, no. But, maybe, at a later stage, after a few years, I may consider it."

As Vikrant and Shweta joined the others outside in the drawing room, all eyes turned to them with anticipation. Vikrant wore a look of satisfaction of having achieved something he had set out for. His mother could see the positive gleam in Vikrant's eyes. Hopefully, Vikrant would not return a bachelor to America. Shweta, on the other hand, looked a little unsure, if not exactly confused. Maybe, Shweta had her doubts which needed to be cleared. All in all, the atmosphere was pregnant with expectations.

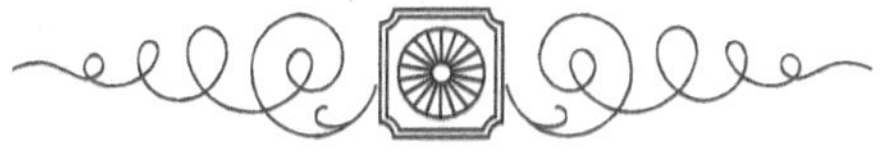

II

On the next day, there was an animated discussion at Vikrant's residence between Vikrant, his parents, his maternal aunt, and the 'facilitator' aunt concerning the merits of Shweta's proposal. Mind you, 'Shweta's proposal', and not 'Shweta'. In arranged marriages in India, the individual merits of the boy and the girl alone are not relevant; there are a whole lot of other factors that are taken into consideration before a proposal is accepted. For instance, a girl who is otherwise perfectly suitable will be rejected if her paternal aunt's brother-in-law's father-in-law had been convicted of murder. So, you see, all proposals in arranged marriages in India go through minute scrutiny on issues not necessarily concerning the boy or the girl.

Let's examine the factors that were considered for Shweta's proposal:

1. **Physical appearance**: In arranged marriages in India, physical appearance, especially for girls, plays a pivotal role. Indians' obsession with fair complexion is well known; no wonder fairness creams are a multi-crore business in

India. So, a girl with a fair complexion always has better prospects in the Indian marriage market. A fair-complexioned girl with a Monica Lewinskyesque face would, therefore, stand a better chance than a slightly darker girl with Halle Berryesque features. In India, the colour of the skin is more important than sharp features. However, when it comes to height, Indian boys are not too choosy. They are happy to be paired with short girls; maybe it is due to the precedent set by Amitabh Bachchan-Jaya Bhaduri. Or, is it that Indian boys want their wives to look up to them, whilst they themselves look down upon them (pun intended)? Whatever the reason, Indian girls need not worry about their height or the lack of it. But, the weight of the girl does carry a lot of weight in the Indian marriage market. Of course, boys would not generally expect to get girls with figures like Jane Fonda, Zeenat Aman, Jenifer Lopez or Bipasha Basu, but being overweight is definitely not going to work in the Indian marriage market. Somehow, Indian boys do show a preference for thin (not to be confused with 'slim') girls.

Shweta was neither too fair nor dark. You could say that she was reasonably fair. She was about 5' 6" tall, reasonably tall by Indian standards. Shweta was medium-built and neither too thin nor overweight. She had sufficiently long hair and sharp features. From Vikrant's mother's point of view, Shweta was perfectly presentable in society as her '*bahu*'. Since Shweta could be categorised as 'good-looking' by Indian standards, Vikrant also approved of her. So, Shweta passed the first test of physical appearance.

2. **Academic Qualification**: There was a time in India when the academic qualifications of girls were hardly relevant. However, with the economic progress that India has made, the academic qualification of girls is not only important in urban India but also a relevant factor to be considered in rural India. If the woman is educated, it has a marked positive effect on the prevailing culture and values at home and the upbringing of children. By educating a girl, we contribute to the overall progress of our country.

   Shweta held an M.A. in English Literature and was employed in the teaching profession. She had already expressed to Vikrant her desire to pursue her PhD in America and join a university as faculty. So, on that count also Shweta passed with flying colours.

3. **Family background**: As mentioned earlier, family background plays a very important role in Indian arranged marriages. In India,

a marriage is not just a union between the bride and groom but their respective families. The compatibility and social standing of both families are thoroughly considered to ensure that this new union benefits from harmonious relationships.

Shweta's family background was commensurate with that of Vikrant's, and there was no problem on that issue.

4. **Status:** In Indian arranged marriages, the social position of the respective families of the bride and bridegroom is always of vital importance. Indians are status-conscious—the British have left behind the legacy of '*burra-sahibs*'—and when it comes to marriage, they become even more status-conscious. Intertwined with the issue of social status is that of economic status. We can even say that the economic status of a family determines its social status. So, in India, alliances are formed between families having equivalent status. To give a few illustrations: if the boy is residing in a 3 BHK flat, the girl is expected to be residing at least in a 2 BHK flat; a 1 BHK would not be acceptable. Similarly, if the boy drives around town in a BMW, the girl's family is at least expected to own a Skoda; a Maruti Swift or Hyundai i20 would not be comparable. If one party in the alliance is

economically weaker than the other, it is always looked down upon. If the unfortunate party happens to be that of the bride, then she has to endure the barbs and taunts of her in-laws. Therefore, arranged marriages usually take place between families enjoying equal status.

Now, Shweta's father held a top managerial position at a financial institution. On the other hand, Vikrant's father was a successful businessman, although he had previously been employed by an MNC. Referring to Shweta's family, when Vikrant's mother said, "*Hamare barabarwale hain*", it succinctly summarised the entire issue of the compatibility of the status of either party.

5. **Caste/Community:** The single most important criterion at the root of factors considered in Indian arranged marriages is undoubtedly the caste and community to which the respective parties belong. Even matrimonial advertisements in newspapers are classified based on caste and community. How advertisements can be placed calling for proposals from prospective brides and bridegrooms is difficult to fathom. Advertisements for 'House for sale', 'Flat to let', 'Car on hire', 'Piano for sale', or even 'Puppies for sale' are understandable, but 'brides' and 'bridegrooms' beat all rationale as if brides

and bridegrooms were chattel. So be it. As far as community as a criterion is concerned, it is quite understandable. After all, associated with every community are particular customs, food habits, ways of dressing, specific festivals, certain cultures, and languages. You can safely say that your way of life is determined by the community to which you belong. But then again, it can be argued whether it is not enough to be an Indian or, for that matter, just being human. After all, life is all about adjustments and married life even more so.

When it comes to arranged marriages in India, caste is one of the most fundamental issues. Even otherwise, caste is a very sensitive issue in the Indian social milieu. Actually, after gaining Independence, the Indian Government should have endeavoured to oust the caste system prevalent in India. In fact, the learned framers of our Constitution did envisage a casteless Indian society. But unfortunately, successive governments and every political party in India have perpetuated the caste system for obvious political gains. Today, caste is no longer just a social issue; it has become a political issue. Today, all government action is determined by political considerations and vote-bank politics, and caste is no stranger to such political largesse.

To begin with, Shweta and Vikrant belonged to the same caste and community. So, in the case of Shweta and Vikrant, caste and community were non-issues, really.

6. **Horoscopes:** It's been almost four decades since man landed on the moon, but even today, some conservative and orthodox families insist on studying the horoscopes of the prospective bride and groom before the alliance is accepted. Such people have more faith in the '*rahus*', '*ketus*', and '*mangliks*' rather than human traits. If a marriage is doomed, it would be because of human frailties rather than the positions of stars. The success of any relationship depends on human nature and attributes like kindness, egotism, attitude, understanding, compassion, honesty, discipline, etc., and marriage is no exception to this. Marriages do not succeed or fail because of forecasts and predictions based on horoscopes but because of factors innately connected with human nature and behaviour. Every person is a complex being, and for two people to live together happily, it would take a lot more effort on either side than simply the matching of two pieces of paper. In India, some marriages take place only because of the matching of horoscopes. It is believed that favourable horoscopes will take care of all future obstacles and ensure a trouble-free and

happy married life. Now, this is incredulous. Horoscopes have no role to play in an age of scientific reasoning and rational thinking. At times, the 'non-matching' of horoscopes is used as a euphemism for rejecting a proposal not found suitable otherwise.

Although Vikrant's family was educated, modern, and progressive, his mother had insisted on getting his and Shweta's horoscopes matched by their family astrologer. Ironically enough, most Indian families, though educated and progressive, often consult astrologers when it comes to taking important decisions in life like marriage, shifting residence, investing in real estate, foreign travel, and the like. While insisting upon the matching of horoscopes, Vikrant's mother had succinctly expressed her thoughts, "*Dil ko tassalli ho jayegi*". Coincidentally and fortunately, their horoscopes did match.

That sums up the factors that were considered in Shweta's proposal, and on all counts, the outcome was positive. It now seemed that Vikrant's search for a bride would end at Shweta's door. After due deliberation, Vikrant's family finally concluded that Shweta was the right girl for Vikrant. In other words, she was 'wife material'.

On the other hand, Shweta's family was also seriously considering Vikrant's proposal. As mentioned before, it is always the boy's prerogative to select or reject the girl, but Shweta's parents, educated and progressive as they were, would definitely not push her into an unsuitable alliance.

So, let's see the factors that were considered about Vikrant's proposal:

1. **Physical appearance:** In arranged marriages in India, the physical appearance of boys is not of much consequence. Girls are expected to be beautiful, but boys can be average. In fact, in India, you'll find many mismatched couples where the girl is distinctly much better looking than the boy. Whereas a boy is entitled to dream of getting a beautiful wife, a girl is not entitled to dream of getting a handsome husband; she is only supposed to dream of getting a rich husband. So, that's the norm: a beautiful wife and a rich husband; never mind if he's ugly.

   Vikrant was what is popularly known in India as wheatish-complexioned. He was close to 6' tall, well-built, and reasonably good-looking. He could well be called 'handsome' by Indian standards. So, Vikrant was more than acceptable on that count.

2. **Academic qualification / Occupation / Income:** In Indian arranged marriages, the most important attributes for a boy are his academic qualifications, occupation, and income. A good academic qualification leads to a good job or professional employment, which in turn ensures a sound income. Boys with good educational qualifications and impressive job profiles are highly sought after in the Indian marriage market. It is believed that such boys will ensure a good life (read 'materialistic') for their wives.

   Vikrant, of course, being a software engineer employed in America, was more than qualified to be a 'good husband'.

3. **Family background:** As stated earlier, family background is a relevant factor for the families of both the bride and the bridegroom. From the boy's point of view, the girl should have a good family background because, after marriage, she's going to be a part of the boy's family. From the girl's point of view, the boy should have a good family background because, after marriage, she will leave her family and reside with the boy's family. In India, the idea of the bride and bridegroom setting up an independent home after marriage is not widely appreciated. Often, the bridegroom is reluctant

to live apart from his parents after his marriage. Now, if the bride can leave her parents and go to reside with her husband after marriage, why can't the bridegroom leave his parents and reside separately with his wife? Simply saying that this is a custom in India is not enough. In most cases, the boys are not men enough and are simply over-grown mamma's boys. That's why the drama that plays out in most Indian homes of an overbearing mother-in-law lording it over her daughter-in-law is the direct result of the timidity of such mamma's boys, who are not even men enough to protect their own wives (newly married in most cases) from their own bossy mothers. Period.

At the cost of repetition, Vikrant's family background was commensurate with that of Shweta's. In other words, Shweta would be happy being a part of Vikrant's family.

4. **Status:** As already stated, in arranged marriages, it is necessary that both parties enjoy equal status, both social and economic. Referring to Shweta's family, Vikrant's mother had said, "*Hamare barabarwale hain*" There was no reason for Shweta's family to think any differently about Vikrant's family.

5. **Caste/Community:** From the point of view of the girl, the caste and community of the

boy's family assume a lot of significance. After marriage, the girl is going to reside with the boy's family. So, she has to adjust to the food habits, customs, dress sense, culture, etc., of the boy's family. In other words, she has to adopt the way of life of the boy's family. If the way of life in which the girl has been brought up is very different from that of the boy's family, it becomes very difficult for her to adjust after marriage. To illustrate the point—if the girl is used to dressing casually, like in jeans and T-shirts, before marriage, and after marriage, she is forced to wear sarees and compulsorily cover her head in the presence of elders, she is bound to feel claustrophobic.

To repeat, Shweta and Vikrant belonged to the same caste and community, so there were no issues on that count.

6. **Horoscopes:** It may be reiterated that human beings are complex by nature and human relations complicated. Merely matching horoscopes does not ensure a happy married life. Compatibility of the couple is key.

Shweta's family was not one to believe in horoscopes. But, since Vikrant's mother had insisted on getting the two horoscopes matched, Shweta's family went along with it. After all, in Indian arranged marriages, the bride's parents often have no alternative but to go along and accept the demands—not requests, mind you—made by the bridegroom's family in the interest of their daughter's happy married life. That such appeasement is no guarantee that their daughter will enjoy a trouble-free married life is another matter. On the contrary, such appeasement often leads to a surge in the demands made by the '*ladkewales*'. Anyway, the horoscopes of Vikrant and Shweta matched.

After much consideration, Shweta's family decided that Vikrant's proposal should be accepted, that is, if Vikrant would accept Shweta's proposal in the first place. Shweta's parents were hoping that Vikrant would accept her proposal so that Shweta would marry into a good family.

III

When Vikrant's mother called up Shweta's mother the next day and conveyed that they had accepted Shweta's proposal, Shweta's mother's happiness knew no bounds. That Shweta was getting a good husband was not so much the reason as it was the idea of announcing to relatives, friends, and neighbours that Shweta had secured a good husband. Mothers of Indian brides often go all over town announcing that their daughters have married very good husbands, that the husband is doing too well, his father is a big shot, his mother is a lovable lady, and generally, how their daughters are fortunate to have been able to marry into such well-to-do families. The happiness expressed by the bride's mother is directly proportional to the prosperity of the bridegroom's family. On the other hand, the bridegrooms' mothers are ecstatic to flaunt their would-be daughter-in-law in society, especially if the bride is exceptionally beautiful. In this system of Indian arranged marriages, everyone from the bride and bridegroom's parents to their relatives, friends, neighbours, acquaintances and society, in general, are more influenced by extraneous considerations in judging the merits of the matrimonial alliance rather than laying due emphasis on the interpersonal relationship and compatibility between the bride and bridegroom. But, then again, how could anybody consider the compatibility of the bride and bridegroom when they hardly know each other? Amazing? No, this is just ridiculous.

Vikrant had just three more weeks at his disposal. It was decided to have the wedding after two weeks; that gave only a fortnight to make all the arrangements. There were a whole lot of things to be done - from deciding the guest list, sending invites, booking the marriage venue, arranging catering, deciding the menu, organising *Sangeet, Mehndi* and other programmes, getting Shweta's trousseau ready in time for the marriage, to arranging gifts for the guests. With a two-week deadline and a definitive task to be achieved, what was required was akin to a Disaster Management Force that would work with military precision. Comparing a wedding to a disaster might sound paradoxical, but the efficient skills required to manage them successfully are identical. Managing Big Fat Indian Weddings is no less a task than handling a disaster. This has precisely given rise to a new breed of professionals who handle all the nitty-gritty of elaborate Indian weddings— the 'wedding planners'. The 'facilitator' aunt introduced Shweta's parents to one such wedding planner, 'Dream Weddings'. The wedding planner assured Shweta's parents that they would live up to their name and put up an impressive show, though time was at a premium. The assurance from the wedding planner did much to allay the anxiety of Shweta's parents. In India, arranging a wedding is traditionally the responsibility of the bride's father. In most cases, the bridegroom's party refuses to share the financial burden of the ceremony, and the bride's father is made to bear the entire expense. Again, the idea is that it is the bride's parents who are keen on getting their daughter married, while the bridegroom is doing them a favour by actually marrying their daughter. That's why the bride's parents go out of their way to ensure that their daughter's wedding goes off without a hitch, that all the wishes of the bridegroom's party are catered to, that the bridegroom's party have no cause for complaint whatsoever. All this is done to ensure that their daughter is treated well after the marriage and that she is not unduly harassed as a result of certain alleged unfulfilled desires of the bridegroom's party at the time of the wedding. In their quest to ensure a dream wedding for their daughter, many parents of Indian brides spend far beyond their means, resulting in them paying off debts for years, long after the wedding is over. It's high time we bring about gender equality in sharing wedding expenses.

Indian weddings have undergone a complete change from the community-specific, comparatively modest affairs they once were. Economic liberalisation has led to the emergence of a burgeoning middle class with high disposable incomes and an eagerness to announce to the world that "we have arrived." And what better occasion to make this statement than a wedding? The degree of ostentation at a wedding has become the new indicator of the economic status and prosperity levels of the hosts.

....

Let's consider the specific manner in which Indian weddings have changed over a period of time.

1. **Wedding Invitation:** Earlier, wedding invitation cards used to be quite predictable, with the draft language often supplied by the printer himself. In fact, some communities printed their wedding invitations in a typical manner. Those who wanted theirs to be different from the run-of-the-mill ones used handmade paper with embossing to make a style statement. Today, wedding invitation cards have evolved to become much more than just that; they are supposed to convey much more than a wedding invitation. Firstly, the exclusivity of the wedding invitation card conveys the prosperity level of the hosts, as exclusive wedding invitations do cost a significant amount. Secondly, an expensive wedding invitation card is often seen as a sure sign of the pomp and grandeur of the upcoming wedding ceremony.

2. **Wedding Venue:** In India, for a long time, marriage ceremonies were conducted in

community-specific, owned, and managed marriage halls. Some of these halls had earned a reputation for themselves, and having a marriage ceremony held at such venues was considered quite prestigious. Some of the most sought-after marriage halls used to be booked almost a year in advance. Today, air-conditioned banquet halls are preferred over traditional marriage halls. Earlier, the rich and famous always opted for five-star hotels as wedding venues. Today, destination weddings have become a symbol of social status. So, the well-heeled types select exotic wedding venues from Goa to Rajasthan and Mauritius to Pattaya for their nuptials. Some, with big fat wallets, even go to the extent of tying their knots on a yacht in mid-sea or on a chartered plane in mid-air.

3. **Wedding Menu**: For generations, every Indian community had its traditional wedding menu, and guests always knew what to expect. So much so that some guests would decide in advance to hold *jalebi* or *gulab-jamun* eating competitions at the wedding. With the emergence of the buffet system, the traditional wedding menu was replaced by a more cosmopolitan spread. Indian weddings are all about ostentation, and prime attention is always given to the wedding menu. After all, the success of a wedding ceremony is

often judged by whether the appetites of the guests are fully satisfied. Today, the choice of the wedding menu often denotes that the hosts have 'arrived'. So, to begin with, you have a '*Chaat* Corner'. This would be followed by different stalls serving Punjabi, South Indian, Gujarati, and Maharashtrian cuisine. As if that were not enough, there would also be stalls catering to Chinese, Italian, and Mexican cuisines. Earlier, the dessert comprised a single item, maybe ice cream or *kulfi*. Today, the desserts offer a wide choice to the guests; from *jalebis, malpuas* with *rabdi, gulab jamuns* with ice cream to three different kinds of cake. And, at the end of it all, there is the ubiquitous '*Paan* Stall'. With such a wide array of dishes on display, there is bound to be huge food wastage. But then, who cares about food wastage in a developing country like India? People are more concerned about flaunting their wealth on occasions like weddings.

4. **Wedding outfit:** For generations, the wedding outfits of Indian brides and bridegrooms have been quite predictable; brides were adorned in silk sarees and bridegrooms in formal suits. The advantage of such outfits was that they could be used again on other occasions. Today, brides and bridegrooms have a fascination for designer ethnic wear; brides hanker after

designer '*lehengas*' and '*cholis*' for the wedding day, while bridegrooms go all over town for the perfect '*sherwani*'. Clothed in such exclusive outfits, the bride and bridegroom resemble a royal couple. And why should they not? After all, it's the most important day of their lives. However, while a saree or a suit can be used even after the wedding is over, the present-day outfits often cannot, for danger of looking over-dressed. Looking good on your wedding day is important, no doubt, but spending a bomb on an outfit which can be worn only once is bad economics.

5. **Beauty treatment**: A visit to the beauty salon prior to the nuptials has always been de rigueur for the bride. Today, not only the bride but also the bridegroom pays the customary visit to the beauty salon prior to that most important day in their lives. While earlier, the beauty treatments were quite basic, today they are not only elaborate but also considerably lighten the wallet. Beauty salons today claim to transform ordinary-looking brides and bridegrooms into film stars, albeit for a day. Everyone dreams of seeing themselves on the screen, and with a video recording of the marriage ceremony, the bride and bridegroom become the 'heroine' and 'hero' for a day.

6. **Bollywood Effect:** Following the box-office success of *'Hum Aapke Hain Kaun'* and *'Dilwale Dulhaniya Le Jayenge'*, all Indian weddings have been influenced by what can be called the 'Bollywood effect'. Whereas earlier '*Sangeet*' was confined mainly to North Indian marriages, today, it has become a pan-Indian ritual. Similarly, the custom of hiding the bridegroom's shoes by the bride's friends or cousins, who then demand money for their return, has now become part of almost all Indian weddings. So, Indian weddings, which used to be about two-day affairs, have now stretched to four-day affairs in the Bollywoodesque style.

7. **Honeymoon:** Even the honeymoon has undergone significant changes over time. Earlier, honeymoon destinations used to be localised—for instance, Mumbaikars often preferred Mahabaleshwar, Delhites chose Shimla, Mussoorie, or Nainital, South Indians thronged to Ooty, and Kolkatans went to Darjeeling. Today, honeymoon destinations can be as varied as Mauritius, Kuala Lumpur, Las Vegas, or Switzerland. If yesterday's choice was Gulmarg, today it's Mt. Titlis.

A common feature that stands out starkly in the aforementioned changes over time is that they all require a generous loosening of the purse strings. However, the question still remains: "Does an ostentatious wedding guarantee a happy married life in the future for the newly married couple?"

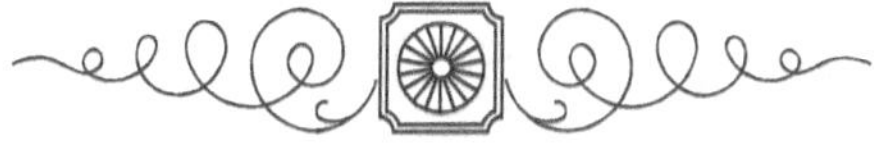

IV

The next day, Vikrant, accompanied by his parents and younger sister, arrived at Shweta's home for the '*Shagun*'. In India, once the girl and the boy have consented to the marriage, the elders in the families choose an auspicious date for the '*Shagun*' ceremony. On the day of '*Shagun*', the groom's mother visits the bride's home with gifts, clothes, betel nut, rice, and incense. Jewellery and sweets are also added to the '*Shagun*'. Acceptance of the '*Shagun*' by the bride signifies her formal consent to become the daughter-in-law of the family. Earlier, the '*Shagun*' symbolised a token, but in today's world of ostentation, the '*Shagun*' may include expensive gifts to impress society about the purchasing power of the parties. After all, '*Shagun*' is the precursor of the grandeur to follow. However, Vikrant's mother avoided going overboard with the '*Shagun*'. Her approach was one of quiet enthusiasm. After all, mothers-in-law avoid giving too much importance to their daughters-in-law to keep them grounded.

Although time was at a premium, Vikrant's mother insisted on having an engagement ceremony performed prior to the actual wedding. Her reasoning was that this being the first wedding in their family, and with Vikrant being the elder sibling, she wanted it to be an elaborate ceremony. Now, in the olden days when there were three or more siblings, a first wedding or last wedding in the family was understandable. But, in today's world, where there are often not more than two siblings, referring to it as the first or last wedding in their family sounds more like a ruse to extract maximum benefits from the bride's family. Shweta's parents, of course, did not want to displease Vikrant's mother. So, they agreed to have an engagement ceremony, with 'Dream Weddings' around to help them with it, at a price, of course.

'*Mangni*' or '*Sagaai*' refers to the engagement ceremony where the girl and boy exchange rings in the presence of elders, family members, and friends. '*Sagaai*' holds significance when the actual wedding is not to be held immediately. Since the engagement ceremony marks an official announcement to society at large about the forthcoming wedding, the boy and girl are then at liberty to date each other officially without being subjected to the barbs of nosey aunts.

In the case of Vikrant and Shweta, the engagement ceremony did not serve any such purpose, as the wedding was to follow shortly. 'Dream Weddings' managed to put on a good show at the engagement ceremony of Vikrant and Shweta, though at short notice. Overall, the engagement ceremony was elegant, although Vikrant's mother would have preferred something more vibrant.

In India, since wedding ceremonies are usually arranged for by the bride's parents, the bridegroom's mother is wont to be fastidious about the nitty-gritty of the event. Nonetheless, the engagement ceremony proceeded smoothly.

The '*Mangni*' or '*Sagaai*' was the harbinger of the wedding that was to follow. Only about a week was remaining and a lot of things were to be attended to; sending out invitation cards, deciding the menu, getting the wedding ensemble ready, booking the wedding venuc, getting the gifts, etc. Thankfully, the wedding planner 'Dream Weddings' was on hand to manage the entire show.

'Dream Weddings' introduced both parties to a design company specialising in wedding cards and gifts. In today's computer age, getting wedding cards printed is no big deal. Gone are the days when the printer would first prepare samples, wait for customer approval after proofreading, and then proceed to print the cards. Today, various samples and designs of cards are displayed on the computer, and various permutations and combinations can be performed digitally. So the customer can select their design swiftly. With the design of the wedding cards selected and approved by Vikrant and Shweta, they were ready to move on to the next task—their wedding outfits.

Getting wedding outfits ready in time for the big day has always been a difficult task. Tailors have never been known to deliver on the appointed date. Fashion designers, the exalted tailors of the modern age, may not be any different. While Shweta preferred to be draped in a traditional silk saree on the most important day of her life, Vikrant would rather that Shweta sport a designer *lehenga* and *choli*, keeping with the modern trend. Not that Vikrant's stint in America had improved his sartorial taste, although he thought otherwise. Sartorial preferences aside, Shweta fell in line with Vikrant's desire. Whether this was a sign of things to come, only time would tell. Vikrant did manage to get his *sherwani* from one of those men's readymade wedding-wear shops. Shweta, on the other hand, had to make several visits to various trousseau boutiques before she could find an outfit that met her approval and, more importantly, Vikrant's liking.

After that came the mandatory visits to the jewellers. In India, just as we have family physicians, we also have a system of family jewellers whom we trust as far as the purity of gold is concerned. Both Shweta and Vikrant had their respective family jewellers who promised to deliver the ornaments in time for the wedding. Traditionally, jewellers in India are not known to keep their word when it comes to delivering the ornaments on time. It takes a lot of coaxing and cajoling before the jeweller finally delivers the ornaments in the nick of time. Maybe that has led to the spurt in over-the-counter sales in big jewellery shops.

In the meantime, 'Dream Weddings' short-listed a few wedding venues. In India, wedding venues, especially the most sought-after, are booked months in advance. So, in the present case, the choice was quite limited. Finally, Vikrant and Shweta chose an air-conditioned banquet hall in a suburban mall. Firstly, it would ensure sufficient availability of parking spaces in a city starved of parking spaces. Secondly, it would obviate the necessity of having extravagant decorations as are usually done in the case of an outdoor wedding setting. It's another thing that 'Dream Weddings' would have preferred an outdoor location to display their skills. So be it; here, the choice was limited, and time was at a premium.

Having finalised the wedding venue, the focus shifted to the wedding menu. Shweta's preference was for an all-Indian menu; she was more concerned about avoiding food wastage. Vikrant, on the other hand, wanted to have a multi-cuisine menu, more concerned as he was about pleasing the guests. So, Vikrant insisted on including a Chinese corner serving fried rice, noodles and manchurian gravy; also, an Italian one dishing out pasta. Thankfully, he did not insist on having an American one serving burgers and fries. Since *jalebis* were part of the main course, Shweta was happy to have *kulfi* for dessert. But Vikrant insisted on having *gulab jamuns*, too, for dessert. Thankfully, he did not also insist on having cakes for dessert. Shweta would not have approved of such indulgence. As it is, fixing a wedding menu is always a ticklish job. Both the bride and the bridegroom's families have their respective preferences, likes and dislikes. Often, the bride's family has to yield to the choice of the bridegroom's family to keep them happy. So much for gender equality.

With a little help from relatives and friends, the guest list was finalised, wedding invitation cards dispatched, some hand-delivered and others emailed. The communication revolution has eased the task of sending invitations, which in the olden days was subject to the vagaries of the postal mail service. With most of the tasks being professionally managed by 'Dream Weddings', things started falling into place as D-Day neared. No bride's parents can breathe easy until the wedding ceremony goes off smoothly, and Shweta's parents were no exception. But 'Dream Weddings' had done much to curb the anxiety of Shweta's parents.

The next item on the agenda was beauty treatment. As mentioned earlier, nowadays, a visit to the beauty salon is a must not only for the bride but also for the bridegroom. Whereas earlier beauty treatments consisted of some basic facial and hair styling, today, they may include everything from manicures and pedicures to skin polishing and skin tightening. Some with overflowing wallets and overwhelming desires even undergo cosmetic procedures like nose jobs, smile correction, and breast augmentation. Whilst earlier, a beauty treatment would entail a visit to the neighbourhood beauty salon, today, it would require visits to a hair stylist, a skin expert, a dentist, and maybe a cosmetic surgeon. Shweta visited her regular neighbourhood beautician for her usual beauty treatment; nothing special or extraordinary. Vikrant, on the other hand, sought out the big names for his hairstyle, facial treatment, manicure, pedicure, and dental treatment, so that he could confidently flash that million-dollar smile on the D-Day.

❧

A couple of days before the ceremonies began, Vikrant headed off to a weekend resort with his friends for what is known as a 'bachelor's party'. Now, what is the reason behind having these bachelor's parties? The most oft-repeated reason is that since, post-marriage, the boy is going to forgo most of the freedoms he enjoyed as a bachelor, he would like to enjoy that one last bash with his bachelor friends to experience freedom as a bachelor for one last time. Actually, if anybody needs to enjoy and savour the freedom of being single for one last time, it is the girl rather than the boy. After marriage, the girl is going to leave her parents' home for the home of her husband; she has to adapt to a new environment and new people; she has to follow the way of life, discipline, food habits, and dress sense as prescribed in her husband's home. It is the girl who is going to lose most of the freedoms that she enjoyed prior to her marriage rather than the boy. Most Indian husbands consider themselves to be the bosses at home and expect their wives to follow their diktats. Add to that an overbearing mother-in-law, and you can guess whose freedom is in jeopardy. So, if anybody needs to party before the wedding, it's the girl, for it's her freedom that is going to be at stake post-marriage. Instead of the boy having a 'bachelor's party', the girl needs to have a 'spinster's party', where she can really let her hair down and enjoy the last vestige of freedom as a spinster. The 'bachelor's party' is nothing more than just another opportunity for the boy to enjoy a 'booze party' with his friends and justify the same. Period.

The rituals in a Hindu wedding vary widely. Pre-wedding and post-wedding rituals and celebrations differ by region, preferences, or the resources of the groom, bride, and their families. They can range from one-day to multi-day events. Nowadays, those with fat wallets and an urge to display their wealth, whether ill-gotten or otherwise, opt for Bollywood-style weddings; they want to recreate "*Hum Aapke Hain Kaun*" in real life. So, today, leaving aside regional rituals, what has emerged is a pan-India, multi-day wedding celebrations, as are seen in Bollywood films.

In keeping with this trend, Shweta and Vikrant's wedding ceremonies began with the '*Sangeet*'. The *Sangeet* ceremony is held in the houses of the bride and groom separately and consists of music, dance, and fun.

The bride's friends revel in teasing her about her future husband. Elders of the house sing traditional songs and bless the bride.

Shweta was initially reticent, but once the mood picked up, she too indulged in the fun and dance that accompanied the '*Sangeet*'. Vikrant, on the other hand, was at his boisterous best and entertained the guests with some Shammi Kapoor-style dance moves. Music, dance, fun, along with good food—what more could the guests ask for at a '*Sangeet*'?

The '*Sangeet*' was followed by the '*Mehndi*'. On this day, the bride is ceremoniously decorated in body art called *Mehndi*. The body art is produced from a mixture of henna and turmeric and symbolises 'the awakening of inner light'. Female guests are invited to participate in the *Mehndi* function that is marked with music and dance.

Shweta was decorated with *Mehndi* on her hands and feet. The intricate designs of the *Mehndi* added to her personality and enhanced the beauty of her fingers and feet. For a woman, her fingers and feet play a pivotal role in enhancing her beauty. It can be a big put-off if a woman is good-looking, but her fingers and feet are not well-cared-for and shabby. Conversely, a woman with ordinary looks can be quite appealing if she has well-maintained fingers and feet. Along with Shweta, her friends and cousins also got themselves decorated with *Mehndi*. That is the general practice. At any Indian wedding, eligible young women decorated with *Mehndi* definitely cause a flutter amongst the eligible young men.

The '*Haldi*' ceremony is held a day prior to the wedding, in the houses of the bride and groom separately. Freshly ground turmeric, mixed with fragrant extracts of jasmine and sandalwood, is believed to impart a natural glow to the bride and groom. The bride and groom are not supposed to leave their houses until the day of the wedding ceremony. Shweta began to glow even more upon the application of *Haldi*; she almost looked like a model straight out of an advertisement for a leading turmeric Ayurvedic cream brand. Apart from turmeric, Shweta's glow may have had much to do with her anticipated marital bliss. Vikrant, on the other hand, considered the *Haldi* ceremony to be nothing more than an occasion for fun and frolic.

As the D-Day, or rather the W-Day, arrived, there was hectic activity in both households. The atmosphere in Shweta's home was pregnant with excitement, coupled with anxiety. In India, it is the responsibility of the bride's parents to see that the marriage ceremony passes off smoothly without any glitches since the rituals are conducted at the bride's place. But placing the entire responsibility of the marriage ceremony on the bride's parents is unfair because, as mentioned earlier, the boy is in as much need of getting married as the girl. Then, why this burden on the bride's parents? It is time for educated and progressive young men to take a stand on this issue; simply taking refuge behind the excuse that this is an age-old practice will not suffice. Period.

Needless to mention, the atmosphere at Vikrant's home was very jovial, with Vikrant being teased about the impending '*suhaag raat*'. The whole idea of marriage in India revolves around the '*suhaag raat*' or the wedding night, where the newlyweds are supposed to experience their first act of coitus. The whole idea of this '*suhaag raat*' has been largely romanticised by Bollywood films; ironically, Bollywood films leave much to the viewers' imagination, unlike Hollywood films, which leave hardly anything to the viewers' imagination. In reality, Indian wedding rituals would leave the newly wedded couple so fatigued that, at the end of it all, they'd rather drop dead in bed than indulge in sexual activity like some sex-starved maniacs. But, most Indians are indeed sex-starved. In India, sex is taboo. Surprising, isn't it, for the world's second most populous country? In India, marriage is considered sacred; thus, sex outside marriage is viewed as sacrilege. Ironic, isn't it, for a country that gave the world the '*Kama Sutra*'? Or, for that matter, in a country that hosts Khajuraho? Sex between two consenting adults is a very natural thing. Consensual sex is a natural phenomenon, but by adopting a regressive mentality towards sex, Indians have only left themselves sex-starved and more prone to offences like stalking, voyeurism, and molestation, if not rape. Take the case of prohibition; you impose prohibition, and the urge to drink increases because it is a forbidden pleasure. You do away with prohibition, and the urge to drink disappears because it is no longer forbidden. The same is the case with sex; once it ceases to be forbidden, many of the sexual offences against women could be curtailed. By restricting sex within marriage, Indian marriages often run into rough weather due to sexual incompatibility between the married couple. Period.

Vikrant arrived at the wedding venue seated atop a white mare in a wedding procession known as '*Baraat*', accompanied by friends, relatives, and family members, with music played by a brass band and dancing by family members and friends throughout the procession.

Shweta looked beautiful, bedecked as she was in a traditional silk saree and gold jewellery that enhanced her personality. Vikrant, on the other hand, appeared every bit the stately groom in an embroidered silk '*Churidar-Kurta*'.

As mentioned earlier, the rituals in a Hindu wedding vary widely. Nevertheless, there are a few key rituals common in Hindu weddings: *Kanyadaan*, *Panigrahana*, and *Saptapadi*, which are respectively the gifting away of the daughter by the father, voluntarily holding hand near the fire to signify union, and taking seven steps, where each step includes a vow/promise to each other, before the sacred fire.

Shweta's father performed her '*Kanyadaan*'. Here, the father asks the groom to not fail the girl in his pursuit of *dharma* (moral and lawful life), *artha* (wealth), and *kama* (love). The groom promises to the bride's father that he shall never fail her in his pursuit of *dharma, artha*, and *kama*. While Shweta's father performed the ritual with the emotional sanctity it deserved, Vikrant's approach to the goings-on appeared to be one of amusement.

It was followed by the '*Panigraha*' or the '*Panigrahana*', which is the 'holding the hand' ritual as a symbol of the impending marital union between the bride and the groom.

Next came the '*Saptapadi*', the most important ritual of Vedic Hindu weddings, representing the legal part of Hindu marriage. The word '*Saptapadi*' means 'seven steps'. After tying the *Mangalsutra*, the newlywed couple takes seven steps around the holy fire, known as *Saptapadi*. Here, traditionally, the bride's *saree* is tied to the groom's *kurta*. He leads her in seven steps around the fire as the priest chants the seven blessings or vows for a strong union. By walking around the fire, they are agreeing to these. With each step, they throw small bits of puffed rice into the fire, representing prosperity in their new life together. This is considered the most important part of the ceremony; it seals the bond forever.

He leads her around four times, and for the last three steps, the bride leads the groom around the sacred fire. It is believed that when a married couple takes seven

'*Pheras*' together, their married life will be happy for a long time. The couple takes vows and pledges their commitment to each other for their entire lives.

The seven steps/vows in the Hindu wedding means:

1. The couple takes the first step and promises to care for each other and pray for abundant blessings and prosperity in their life.

2. In the second step, the couple promises and prays to the Gods to bless them with physical and mental strength and to lead a healthy married life.

3. During the third step, they promise to protect and increase their wealth by proper means.

4. With the fourth step, the bride and groom pledge to share both happiness and sadness together.

5. With the fifth step, the couple promises to be responsible and care for their children.

6. The sixth step is taken by the couple to always be together.

7. And while taking the last seventh step, they promise to be truthful and trustworthy to each other and pledge to be united always in friendship and harmony.

After the seventh step, the two become man and wife. Shweta was trying to understand the meaning and significance behind each vow as recited by the priest. On the other hand, Vikrant treated the rituals merely as a formality that had to be completed. For Shweta, the marriage ceremony was a very sacred and significant moment in her life; it was going to change her life forever. For Vikrant, the marriage ceremony was all about fun and entertainment; he did not believe in the sanctity of the rituals.

Upon the conclusion of the wedding rituals, the guests in attendance were treated to lunch. Then came the time for '*Bidaai*' or for the bride to leave for the groom's home. This is the most emotional part of an Indian arranged marriage. A marriage is supposed to be the happiest event in a girl's life. Then, why shed tears at '*Bidaai*'? The reason is obvious – the girl has to leave her parental home, where she was born and brought up, and go on to live with the groom's family, whom she hardly knows, forget loves. Bollywood, too, has done its bit to fuel the melodrama attached to '*Bidaai*' with song sequences like "*Chhod babul ka ghar, mohe pi ke nagar, aaj jaana pada*." In reality, too, '*Bidaai*' scenes in Indian arranged marriages are typically played out, with the bride, her mother, sisters, and close friends hugging one another and shedding buckets of tears while the groom looks around indifferently. The single most important factor that makes '*Bidaai*' such a tear-jerker in Indian arranged marriages is the fact that the bride is forced to go and live with a man she hardly knows. Everyone accepts this unquestionably as being part of a girl's fate. Aren't Indian girls entitled to marry for love? Shweta's '*Bidaai*' was no different; it played out typically with Shweta hugging her mother, sister, friends, and aunts tearfully while Vikrant looked around indifferently, if not exactly amused.

The '*Bidaai*' is followed by '*Grihapravesh*'. After the wedding is complete, the bride leaves for the groom's home, where the family members of the groom welcome the newlywed couple in a ritual known as '*Grihapravesh*'—homecoming/entry. A Hindu bride is considered a harbinger of wealth and prosperity; therefore, '*Grihapravesh*' consists of a ritual where the bride is required to push an urn full of rice placed at the entrance of the groom's house inwards with her right foot, signifying an abundant future, and taking the first steps in her new home with feet soaked in '*Kum kum*'. Shweta's '*Grihapravesh*' was no different.

The marriage ceremony had passed off smoothly and as planned. Shweta's parents were relieved, and Vikrant's parents were happy. That's how Indian arranged marriages are; happiness is the prerogative of the groom's parents, while for the bride's parents, the entire marriage ceremony is one big task, test, endeavour, or responsibility, whatever one may call it, that has to be successfully completed and/or fulfilled. Whoever said that a marriage is the union between two equal partners had obviously not seen how Indian arranged marriages are played out.

The wedding reception followed the next day. Often, only relatives and close friends are invited to witness the nuptials, and therefore, a reception is held where friends, neighbours, and acquaintances are invited to bless the newlywed couple. In India, there is a practice of inviting all and sundry to a wedding reception, so much so that often the guest invited is not known personally to the newlywed couple and vice versa. This can lead to awkward situations. Take a case where the groom's father invites a business acquaintance who has never met the groom to the wedding reception. If the groom's father is not present on the stage when the business acquaintance goes up to greet the groom, what is he supposed to do? Should he introduce himself? What if the groom has never heard of him before? This happens because everyone, from the groom's parents and siblings to the bride's parents and siblings, has their own individual list of guests to be invited. Half of them may not even be known to the bride and the groom.

Apart from the awkward situations mentioned above, an overflowing presence of guests at a wedding reception can not only cause inconvenience in the circulation of people but also cause much inconvenience in the dining area; guests can end up with soiled clothes with too many people jostling for space with a plateful of food in hand. A more appropriate guest list would include only those persons who are personally known to the bride or the groom. Apart from avoiding any awkward situations and inconvenience to the guests, it would do much to curtail the expenses being foisted upon the bride's parents. In India, the groom's parents often go overboard with their guest list, and with a view to please them, the bride's parents often end up with overrun debts. Why should a bride's marriage be the cause of her parents' indebtedness? A marriage is a very personal occasion for the bride, the groom, and their family members. At most, their relatives and close friends may be invited to grace the occasion, but otherwise, the world has nothing to do with anybody's marriage. It is time we Indians do away with the practice of inviting all and sundry for wedding ceremonies and curtail the much avoidable wedding expenses. After all, does an extravagant wedding guarantee a happy married life to the bride and the groom?

A banquet hall being the reception venue, the decorations were not exactly extravagant; the interior design of the banquet hall itself was good enough. The dinner menu was varied but not excessive. The menu was in keeping with the wishes of both Shweta and Vikrant. Shweta looked resplendent in her designer *lehenga* and *choli*, though, as mentioned earlier, she would have preferred a traditional silk saree for the reception as well. Shweta carried herself with poise throughout the evening and endeared herself to the guests with her enchanting smile. Vikrant looked handsome in his *sherwani*, but he would have appeared stately had he opted for a suit instead. With his swagger, Vikrant came across as a typical America-based Indian. In arranged marriages, the groom often tries to create an impression before the bride's guests that, in him, the bride's family has netted a big catch. Given the Indians' obsession with the US of A, Vikrant could not be blamed for his demeanour. The food was such as would appeal to a gourmand. All the guests left satisfied, having enjoyed a hearty meal. Guests always rate the success of a wedding ceremony based on the goodies that they get to savour. If all the other paraphernalia at a wedding ceremony is a cut above the ordinary, but the food fails to satiate the taste buds of the guests, then the wedding would invariably be labelled as so-so. But, pamper the taste buds of the guests, and the wedding is immediately dubbed a success; shortcomings otherwise, if any, being conveniently forgotten. Of course, in the present case, 'Dream Weddings' made sure that there would be no cause for any complaint.

As the wedding reception drew to a close, Vikrant's parents were happy that the entire ceremony, from the '*Sangeet*' to the reception, was up to the mark, and the guests had left fully satisfied. Shweta's parents heaved a sigh of relief that the entire ceremony had passed off smoothly, without any glitches, and most importantly, had met the expectations of Vikrant's parents. Vikrant had a look of achievement on his face. What exactly, he wondered, had he achieved? Was it getting married to a girl whom he did not even know existed about a month ago, or was it the idea of being married, per se? In other words, the idea that he now had a wife who would take care of all his needs and even his whims and fancies?

Most Indian husbands are under the misconception that, by merely being husbands, they are in an exalted position and expect to be pampered by their wives. Many of these men have a history of being pampered by their mothers, then being in the exalted position of 'sons', and now expect the same treatment from their wives, continuing in the exalted position of 'husbands'. Most mothers-in-law even give lessons to their newly married daughters-in-law on how they need to pamper their sons/husbands.

Whatever the reason, Vikrant did carry a contented look on his face; Shweta, on the other hand, exhibited a picture of cautious happiness; happy because she was now married to a supposedly well-matched boy and cautious because she did not really know what to expect in the future. Perhaps every girl who has an arranged marriage experiences similar emotions. She is, at once, happy because she is getting a life partner, a bulwark, and also apprehensive because she doesn't really know the boy; not as well as a wife should know her husband. As if living with a person not completely known to her is not enough, she also has to adjust to a new home and a new family, with strange habits, a new set of rules and discipline, and everything. With an arranged marriage tending to get claustrophobic, would there be a window open enough for love to creep in?

After *'Grihapravesh'*, the couple proceeds to their honeymoon. This is the period when newlywed couples take a break to share some private and intimate moments that help establish love in the relationship. This privacy, in turn, is believed to ease the comfort zone towards a physical relationship, which is one of the primary means of bonding during the initial days of marriage.

The term "honeymoon", which refers to the time in which the bride and groom adjust to their new state of matrimony, most likely received its name from a drink known as mead, which, in the early years of England, was served to the bride and the groom at their wedding celebrations and also before retiring every night for a full cycle of the moon. Mead, a fermented liquor with a base made of an abundance of honey, some water, and a few spices, was considered a fertility drink, and its consumption guaranteed the couple offspring.

Today, a honeymoon is a chance for a newlywed couple to get away from the hustle and bustle of everyday life, the stress they encountered from planning their wedding, and the attention they received from family and friends regarding their marriage. It's a time for the two of them to relax and spend some romantic and intimate time together in a very special location.

In cases of arranged marriages, the honeymoon serves the purpose of getting to know one another, for finding out more about your partner in a relaxed environment away from the hustle and bustle of everyday life, hopefully in a beautiful and romantic setting to better enable love to blossom.

That newlywed couples need to share some private and intimate moments together is perfectly understandable, but if we were to look at the purpose that a honeymoon is supposed to serve in the case of arranged marriages, two factors stand out clearly: "getting to know one another" and "enabling love to blossom". Firstly, "getting to know each other" implies that the couple doesn't know one another although they are married. In other words, the boy and the girl first marry each other and then set about the task of getting to know each other because they happen to be married to each other. What happens if they dislike each other or don't approve of one another's habits and/or behaviour after getting to know one another? Secondly, "enabling love to blossom" presupposes that there was no love between the couple when they married each other. To put it differently, the boy and the girl first marry each other, and then force themselves to love each other because they happen to be married to each other. Shouldn't it be the other way around, i.e., marry each other because they love each other? In the natural course, marriage is supposed to follow love, not vice versa. And what happens if, after marriage, the couple is not able to get themselves to love one another? After all, people fall in love; love cannot be forced upon anybody.

Since Vikrant was scheduled to fly to America shortly, there was no time for a long-range honeymoon. So, Vikrant and Shweta could only manage a very brief honeymoon to a nearby weekend getaway. Soon after the honeymoon, Vikrant left for America. Shweta was to join Vikrant in a couple of months as soon as her visa formalities were completed. Vikrant left with a definite sense of achievement; after all, just about a month ago, he had arrived in India for 'bride-searching', and now here he was, returning to America, a much-married man. Shweta, on the other hand, was bewildered by the sudden change in her marital status, all within a span of a month. She was unsure what emotion she was meant to feel; was she to feel sad because her partner of about three weeks had left for America, or was she to feel happy that she could spend a few more weeks with her parents before she flew to America? She was confused, whether to feel sad as she would be leaving India in a couple of months or whether to be happy that she would be flying to America – every overambitious Indian's dream destination – to be with her husband.

V

TWO YEARS LATER

Shweta was back at her parents' house. Now, wait, please don't jump to any conclusions; Shweta was not expecting a visit from the stork. Even otherwise, Indians are nosy people, and when it comes to newlyweds, as soon as the first wedding anniversary is celebrated, everyone from family members and relatives to friends, neighbours, and acquaintances becomes curious to know whether there is any 'good news'. Hello! Please understand that this entire business of 'good news' is very much a personal matter between a husband and a wife. But, Indians expect the wife to shout from the rooftops that "I'm pregnant!!" and the husband to announce to all and sundry that "I'm going to be a father!!" The inquisitiveness is often accompanied by questioning expressions, raising doubts about the potency or otherwise of the husband and the fertility or otherwise of the wife. At times, the prying can get so intense that it can actually dent the confidence of an otherwise healthy couple. Why can't Indians appreciate that whether and when to have a baby is a personal matter between a married couple, and the world has nothing to do with it? Often, the wife's mother wants the stork to visit her daughter, only to show the entire world that her daughter is healthy and fine. Similarly, the husband's mother looks forward to her daughter-in-law getting pregnant to prove to the entire world that there's nothing wrong with her son. It is as if the entire world is so concerned that it is going to take care of and raise the newborn child. As soon as a married couple begets a child, they are conveniently forgotten by society; otherwise, they are subjected to increasing barbs with the passage of every additional year without any 'good news'. It's time Indians learn to mind their own business and refrain from poking their noses into the personal matters of others.

Unfortunately for Shweta, she was back because her marriage with Vikrant had run into rough weather. What began as a disagreement over minor issues later metamorphosed into major disputes and squabbles. Finally, it all came down to a question of compatibility.

Actually, the problem, if you can call it that, began during the very brief honeymoon itself, before Vikrant flew to America. Like most Indian men, Vikrant was all too eager to jump into bed with Shweta during the honeymoon. For him, Shweta was now his lawfully wedded wife, and that gave him an inalienable right to her person. So, there was no way he was going to America without consummating his marriage; remember, for him, this marriage was all about achievement. For Shweta, though, it was a very delicate situation. She had hardly known Vikrant for about three weeks. In that sense, her relationship with Vikrant was only three weeks old. Now, when it comes to friendship, three weeks would be considered too short a period to consider someone a 'close friend'. Yet, here she was supposed to sleep with a man whom she had hardly known for about three weeks simply because he was her husband. Naturally, Shweta was unable to open up completely to Vikrant, resulting in him feeling somewhat unsatisfied and Shweta embarrassed. What Shweta needed was time to feel comfortable with Vikrant, and time was the only luxury that Vikrant could not afford at that moment. Shweta hoped and believed that things would fall into place once she joined Vikrant in America.

Things began to look up for the newlyweds when Shweta joined Vikrant in America. The initial days were spent setting up their home which, in fact, helped the two of them get closer to each other. Shopping together for their household needs helped them bond. Vikrant introduced Shweta to his group of friends that included boys and girls, Indian, American, and even Chinese. They started having weekend get-togethers, either at someone's place or at a weekend resort. Shweta was trying to adjust to the new way of life. For Shweta, her life had completely changed from what it was back in India. Back in India, Shweta's life had been disciplined, serious, and followed a set routine. Vikrant, on the other hand, was impulsive and often took spontaneous decisions.

As a result, Shweta was never short of surprises. But Shweta took all the surprises in her stride, hoping that she would soon get used to the way of life in America, in general, and the way of life with Vikrant, in particular.

As the novelty of the new relationship began to wear off, irritants started to crop up. Vikrant was as disorganised as Shweta was organised. To begin with, there is no system of domestic help in the USA. Everybody is expected to take care of his or her individual household chores. However, Shweta received no help worth its name from Vikrant in managing the house. Vikrant expected Shweta to manage the domestic chores single-handedly. Even on weekends, Vikrant would rather have outings with friends than spend time with Shweta. After all, the whole idea behind getting a wife during the month-long India visit was that she would cook for Vikrant and take care of his house. Would it then sound harsh to say that Vikrant actually wanted a cook cum maid who would also get into bed with him at night? Not really, because most Indian men treat their wives in a similar fashion. For them, a wife, therefore, is someone who cooks and works for them for free and, in addition, offers sex for free. They fail to appreciate that wives cook and work out of love, and therefore, they, too, need a loving helping hand. For Vikrant, there was a clear segregation of roles—he would go out to work, and Shweta would take care of the house. In short, he would be the economic provider and she, the caregiver.

Fine, but being the economic provider doesn't exempt him from lending a helping hand with the household chores.

Gradually, the bond that had developed between Vikrant and Shweta in their initial days together began to wear thin. Vikrant started spending a major part of the day outside the house. He would leave early and return late. If work did not keep him late at the office, he would visit pubs in the evening with his friends. At times, he would visit a pub alone and gulp a few drinks before proceeding home. There was not much communication between the two of them. Something was missing in their relationship.

Shweta was not exactly a party animal. Initially, she tried to get along with Vikrant's friends, but she was never really into it. While with his friends, she would put up a façade of enjoyment, but she did not quite relish their company. As though she had a choice; she was in a foreign land, with no friends of her own. The first sign that something was not quite right between Vikrant and Shweta came when Shweta started excusing herself from his group of friends. She stayed alone at home while he partied with his friends. Shweta was back with her books for company.

Shweta thought she needed to be productively occupied. She had been a lecturer back in India, and unless she received intellectual stimulation, she would head for a breakdown in America. She, therefore, broached the subject of pursuing higher education in America with Vikrant, but his response was neither enthusiastic nor encouraging. While he didn't explicitly prohibit her from continuing her education, he didn't offer support either, leaving Shweta to make her own decisions. With no help forthcoming from Vikrant, Shweta had to dig into her own resourcefulness to join the university and pursue further education. Since she did not want to depend on Vikrant to sponsor her further studies, she also got a part-time job tutoring undergraduate students at the university.

To say she was happy with these developments would be a misnomer, but Shweta was definitely pleased with the way in which the arrangement was working out. Firstly, it allowed her to do what she loved the most: teaching. Secondly, it permitted her to pursue her dream of doctoral research, and that too, in America. But most importantly, she had won back her freedom and independence which she had surrendered to Vikrant's whims and fancies.

However, as Shweta settled into a more purposeful life in America, the chasm in her relationship with Vikrant grew wider. It was like they were living under the same roof, but there was no affection worth its name between them. They started living separate lives. Vikrant would leave the house in the morning as per his routine and return late at night. Shweta would be engrossed in her academic pursuits. They even stopped having meals together; Shweta would eat dinner at her preferred time at home, while Vikrant often dined out.

The first casualty in this evolving dynamic was communication. There was hardly any meaningful interaction between them. From the beginning itself, Vikrant never had any office talk with Shweta. His policy was, once home, no discussion about office. As a result, Shweta could never become Vikrant's confidante. Thus, the relationship between Vikrant and Shweta could not progress beyond the superficial. Vikrant, therefore, had nothing much to share with Shweta, and though she would have loved to share her experiences with him, he remained indifferent.

The relationship between Vikrant and Shweta was clearly on a downward spiral. Whenever their parents called, both Vikrant and Shweta assured them that things were fine. Shweta, especially, did not want her parents to be worried, so she always painted a picture that she was happy with Vikrant in America. There was no apparent reason for her parents to disbelieve her, especially since she was also pursuing further studies in America.

And then it happened one day. Vikrant was having a shower when his cellular phone rang. Shweta just glanced to see if she knew the caller. It was Jane, an American from Vikrant's group of friends. Since Shweta knew Jane, she answered the call, but before Shweta could say "Hello!" Jane, based on the assumption that it was Vikrant on the other end, blurted out mushy talk that left Shweta astounded. Without losing her composure, Shweta responded, "Jane, it's me, Shweta." A flabbergasted Jane stuttered, "Oh my God! Sshweta, llook I..I..I can explain..." Without waiting any further for Jane's explanation, Shweta disconnected the call.

After showering, Vikrant checked his call records and realised that Jane had called and that the call had been answered. He asked Shweta whether Jane had called. She confronted him with a counter-question, "Vikrant, what's going on between you and Jane? I want to know the truth." Seeing the stern look on Shweta's face and hearing her dour voice, Vikrant knew that the game was up.

Without beating around the bush, Vikrant admitted that he had been having an affair with Jane. Shweta's heart sank, though she had suspected as much. He added that he and Jane had been seeing each other even before the marriage. He had expressed his desire to marry Jane to his parents. While his father was not exactly pleased, he did not object, but his mother was adamant about having a '*desi bahu*'. "No '*firangi*' *bahu* in my house," she had declared. When it became clear that his mother would not accept a white American for a daughter-in-law, Vikrant had to make a choice: either to marry Jane and settle down in America for good or forget Jane and marry an Indian girl, enabling him to join his father's business later. After much deliberation, he decided to go with his mother's wishes. He and Jane decided to remain 'just friends'. In order to absolve himself, Vikrant also explained to Shweta as to how he had made sincere efforts to make their marriage work in the initial stages. Somehow, things had not worked out between them, and he drifted back to Jane. In order to make Shweta feel better, he also told her that she was not to blame and any man would love to have her as a wife. Shweta began to feel like a sacrificial pawn in a game of chess.

Shweta came to the final question, "Did you have sex with Jane?" Vikrant admitted he had had before marriage. On further prodding, he confessed that he had gone back to maintaining physical relations with Jane when his relationship with Shweta had begun to sour. Vikrant was trying to paint a picture of himself as a victim of circumstances.

Now, the marital relationship between Vikrant and Shweta had reached its nadir. After this revelation, there was no way Shweta could share the same house with Vikrant. She moved in with Radha, one of her Indian colleagues, until she completed her thesis. After finishing her academic commitments, Shweta returned to her parents' house in India.

Shweta was fortunate that her parents stood solidly behind her and did not shun their responsibility like parents of most married Indian girls. As unbelievable as it may sound, but in India, some parents do actually consider their daughters to be a 'burden', and getting them married a 'responsibility'. Upon marriage, it is made clear to the daughter that the parents have discharged their responsibility, and the daughter is now resigned to her fate, which may befall her in her matrimonial home. Even if the daughter is subjected to harassment, physical and/or mental, by her in-laws, she is not welcome in her parents' home, for two reasons. Firstly, after getting the daughter married, the responsibility of the parents ceases, and it is for the daughter to adjust to the situation at her matrimonial home. Secondly, the fear of what the society will say if their married daughter were to come back to reside with them. Who is the society to question you? Is the society going to take up the responsibility of your daughter? No, then why care a damn about what the society will say? How many cases have we come across where such unfortunate married girls are left with nowhere to go, nobody to turn to for help and support, and ultimately end up committing suicide? Shweta, fortunately, enjoyed her parents' support.

Two years ago, Shweta was looking forward to a future with Vikrant; now, she was contemplating a future without him.

VI

Whenever relations between spouses become strained, they often degenerate into a blame game. More often than not, it is not the spouses themselves but their parents, relatives, and friends who add fuel to the fire, resulting in a situation where, even if the spouses want to reconcile, their so-called support group does not allow it. The husband and wife may not see each other as adversaries, inasmuch as it is their own lives and future that are at stake. However, for the other players involved, it is akin to a war they must win. For them, victory would be nothing short of a decree of divorce issued by a matrimonial court, where the other side is held guilty for the breakup of the marriage. Thus, the husband's mother could proudly assert, "She was like this only from the beginning; it was all her fault." As if her son was innocent as a child. Similarly, the wife's mother would say, in her daughter's defence, "Unfortunately for us, the boy turned out to be characterless." For them, their daughter is as pure as honey. In the battle of egos between the families of the spouses, ultimately, it is the husband and wife who end up with fractured lives and an uncertain future. No, it is not being suggested, not even for a moment, that the spouses should not go in for a divorce. If the situation warrants, if either of the spouses feels that continuing the marital bond would be injurious to their physical and/or mental well-being, then by all means, the legal remedy of divorce should always be availed of. It's better to be divorced and happy rather than continue to be unhappily married. There is no stigma attached to being a divorcee. The point being made is that, despite their differences, spouses may still want to give each other another chance. After all, breaking up with someone you are so intimately connected with is not easy.

Shweta's mother stopped just short of accusing the 'facilitator' aunt of deliberately pushing forward Vikrant's proposal. She made it appear as though Shweta was a fish who had fallen prey to the bait of Vikrant's proposal, dangled by the 'facilitator' aunt. Then, can we say that an arranged marriage is all about dangling the bait of an attractive marriage proposal before prospective brides and grooms, who fall prey to the publicised claims of the proposal?

On the other side, Vikrant's mother was blaming Shweta for having failed in her duties as an 'Indian' wife. So, what exactly are these duties of an 'Indian' wife? Well, in India, even if a boy is known to have vices, the girl is expected to marry him. It is believed that, after marriage, the boy will turn over a new leaf. If, after marriage, the boy does really manage to rid himself of his vices, it's said that the marriage has worked wonders on him.

However, if the husband continues with his unwelcome indulgences, even after marriage, then the wife gets solely blamed for having failed to wean her husband away from his vices. So, if a proposed husband is habituated to drinking, the girl is not supposed to reject his proposal on that count; she is supposed to marry him and wean him away from his drinking habit after their marriage. Now, if the husband continues to indulge in heavy drinking in spite of his wife's best efforts to prevent him from doing so, it is the wife who is held responsible for having failed in her duty as a wife. In short, what the mother could not prevent her son from doing before his marriage, the wife is supposed to do after her marriage to him. And whilst the mother is not held responsible for her failure in instilling correct values in her son, the wife is answerable for the wrongdoings of her husband. In an arranged marriage, why is the girl expected to compromise her happiness and take over the burden of correcting a wayward husband?

Vikrant's mother, too, believed that, after his marriage to Shweta, the influence of Jane over his life would wane, and since that did not happen, she considered it a failure on the part of Shweta. So, what was Shweta supposed to have done to wean Vikrant away from the seductive charm of Jane? Shweta was Vikrant's real wife, not a reel vamp from some Bollywood flick. By expecting Vikrant to get over Jane soon after his marriage to Shweta, his mother had adopted an oversimplified approach to a very complex issue. Obviously, Vikrant's involvement with Jane was not restricted to mere physical intimacy. So also, to expect Vikrant and Shweta's marital relations to take off on the touchstone of their physical relations was to take a very simplistic view of their marriage. Marital relationships are complex, and arranged marriages, all the more so. But why are arranged marriages so complicated? The genesis of the complications in arranged marriages arises from the manner in which the arranged marriages are, well, arranged. To understand the complexity of arranged marriages, let's take up the marriage of Vikrant and Shweta as a case study.

Now, let us go back to where it all began. Shweta had been short-listed as a prospective bride by Vikrant based on her photograph and other particulars which had been mailed to him by his mother. Needless to say, the clinching factor in short-listing Shweta's proposal was obviously her photograph. Here comes the first basic flaw in arranged marriages: too much importance is given to 'looks'. When one has not even met his/her prospective life partner, 'good looks' become the primary consideration. The thinking is that if the girl is beautiful, she must be otherwise also endowed with attributes of a good wife. Similarly, if the boy is handsome, he must be a gentleman. However, looks can be very deceptive. In the quest for a 'beautiful wife' or a 'handsome husband', people have often ended up with wrong choices and unhappy marriages. Secondly, the thinking is also that, "Since I'm going in for an arranged marriage, I can be choosy. Why should I settle for anything less than a beautiful wife or a handsome husband?" Thus, the basics of selecting a life partner through an arranged marriage are akin to shopping. When people go shopping, they buy only those things that they find attractive. In the same way, in arranged marriages, beautiful girls and handsome boys get 'picked up' first. But if an attractive thing is later found to be useless, it can be discarded. At the most, it would amount to a monetary loss. But what happens if a beautiful girl or a handsome boy is later found to be not suitable or compatible?

So, when Vikrant short-listed Shweta as a prospective wife, what did he know of her other than how she looked, and that too, from her photograph? Nothing. Just imagine; Vikrant had short-listed a girl whom he could possibly marry, even when he had not met her personally. One wouldn't buy even a car, cellular phone, or a wristwatch by simply seeing a photograph. One would normally consider the market reports about the product one wants to buy. This brings us to the next step in the Vikrant-Shweta matrimony.

In arranged marriages, market reports about prospective brides and grooms are made available by the marriage bureaus or the 'facilitator'. And here, too, a marriage bureau may be able to provide only basic information, limited to what is available in its database. A 'facilitator' may be in a position to provide better information if the prospective bride or groom or both are known to her. In the case of newspaper matrimonial advertisements, the nature of the proposal itself rules out any market reports. Since Vikrant's maternal aunt's sister-in-law was the 'facilitator', and Shweta was her friend's neighbour's daughter, the 'facilitator' aunt could provide market reports to both Vikrant and Shweta about each other. But what exactly do these market reports consist of? Well, usually they would not extend beyond the basic information like educational qualifications, job/business information, and family background. However, if the prospective bride and groom are personally known to the 'facilitator', as in the case of Vikrant and Shweta, the 'facilitator' would have personally endorsed their proposal by saying, "I know the boy/girl. He/she is a good boy/girl." The emphasis is on the term 'good'. So, what would 'good' mean in terms of a prospective bride and groom? Well, it would generally mean well-mannered, polite, and obedient - personality traits that are all observed in the public domain. Marriage is a very personal and intimate relationship. A person's behaviour in the public domain can be markedly different from that in private. A highly personal relationship like marriage requires a very high degree of compatibility. Yes, both Vikrant and Shweta qualified to be 'a good boy' and 'a good girl' in the public domain. But was that enough to ensure compatibility between them as a couple?

The information available about a boy or a girl in the marriage market is general information. Without engaging the services of a private detective, one would not be able to ferret out highly personal information about a prospective bride or groom. Even the 'facilitator' aunt was unaware of Jane. And what if she was? Vikrant had decided to end his liaison with Jane and marry an Indian woman. All proposals in arranged marriages have an element of trust built into them. The problem with them is that the trust often borders on blind faith. How many would have the resources or the inclination to have a private detective pursue a matrimonial proposal?

So, when Vikrant decided to consider Shweta's proposal—or vice versa—what did they know about each other? Well, other than a photograph, basic information, and hearsay that she/he is a good girl/boy, nothing more. It was as if they had read and heard market reports about a particular model of a car and had now decided to go visit a dealer to see the model for themselves.

Now, that brings us to the 'girl-seeing programme'. In this case, it was the 'Vikrant seeing Shweta' programme. When a boy goes to 'see' a girl, he is often accompanied by his relatives and, sometimes, even friends. Vikrant, too, was accompanied by his parents, his maternal aunt, and his maternal cousin. To add to the crowd, the 'facilitator' aunt, along with her friend, was already present at Shweta's residence. Why is it necessary? Can't these 'girl-seeing programmes' be a private affair between the boy, the girl, and their respective parents? Or is it some sort of entertainment programme? Besides, the more the number of people, the more the number of opinions. Ideally, what should count is only the opinion of the boy and the girl, and no one else's.

Let us now consider the private conversation between Vikrant and Shweta. In arranged marriages, it is these private conversations between the boy and the girl that often hold the key to sealing the alliance. Both the boy and the girl try to impress each other. But first impressions can often be deceptive. To begin with, Vikrant and Shweta were meeting each other for the very first time. Just imagine you are meeting someone for the very first time in your life, and you have to decide whether you can spend the rest of your life with that person after just one meeting! The conversation between Vikrant and Shweta was nothing beyond the usual, which a boy and a girl meeting each other for the first time would have. Vikrant did most of the questioning, and Shweta did the answering. In these 'girl-seeing programmes', the girl is only supposed to answer the questions asked of her. Any attempt on the part of the girl to counter-question the boy would come across as rebellious. The conversation revolved mostly around their respective interests and pastimes. It was like any other normal conversation. The only hint that the meeting was for matrimonial purposes came when Vikrant questioned Shweta whether she would be able to adjust to the American way of life. Suppose Vikrant and Shweta had met each other otherwise than for prospective matrimonial purposes, they would have had the same conversation, except perhaps the bit regarding Shweta adjusting to the American way of life. The point being made here is, after a first normal friendly meeting, how much did Vikrant and Shweta know each other or understand each other to be able to make the crucial decision that they could spend the rest of their lives with each other? It was a decision of a lifetime to be taken after meeting each other only for a few minutes. One would not take decisions relating to even realty in such a manner.

After the 'girl-seeing programme' comes the part of considering the merit of the proposal. Ideally, only the boy and the girl should consider the suitability or otherwise of the proposal. At the most, their parents can share their opinions with them. But in India, even relatives often voice their opinions, most often uninvitedly. In Vikrant's case, apart from him and his parents, his maternal aunt and the 'facilitator' aunt also participated in considering Shweta's proposal. So, how much did Vikrant know about Shweta, and what exactly went into consideration for Shweta's proposal? The factors considered were physical appearance, academic qualifications, status, family background, caste/community, and horoscopes. Would any one, or more, or all of these factors ensure that Vikrant's marriage with Shweta would be a success? The most crucial factors that were missing were Vikrant 'knowing' Shweta and 'loving' Shweta. Probably, what clinched it for Vikrant was that Shweta came across as a simple, homely, and adjusting type of girl who wouldn't cause much confrontation in Vikrant's life. But then, this was only Vikrant's perception of Shweta.

Now, let's consider the factors that went into the consideration of Vikrant's proposal by Shweta and her parents. The factors were physical appearance, academic qualifications/occupation/income, family background, status, caste/community, and horoscopes. Again, the same question arises: would Shweta be happy with Vikrant as her husband only due to the positive consideration of the aforementioned factors? What about Shweta 'knowing' Vikrant and 'loving' Vikrant? Although Vikrant had appeared to be brash and boisterous, unlike Shweta, she went along with his proposal because she probably thought that she would lead a comfortable life with Vikrant. 'Comfortable' meant smooth and secure.

So, as can be seen, Vikrant and Shweta entered into matrimony only with certain perceptions about each other. Neither really knew nor loved the other.

Now, that brings us to the post-marriage phase. The first stumbling block that Vikrant and Shweta faced after marriage was sex. In arranged marriages, sex has always remained a very ticklish issue. Firstly, the newly married couple is in a very awkward situation—the husband and wife are married to each other but they neither know each other too well nor are they friendly with each other. Secondly, the wife, who has left her parental home and come to reside with her husband, needs time to adjust to the new home, new people, new way of life, and her new husband. Before opening up physically, the wife needs to open up mentally to the new surroundings. At such times, the husband needs to provide emotional support to his newly wedded wife so that she feels comfortable in her new home rather than force himself upon her and cause her emotional distress. As it is, India is a hugely sex-deprived nation, and marriage gives an absolute licence to Indian men to claim their marital rights. Shweta had hardly known Vikrant for three weeks when they got married. They could hardly be expected to be good friends in that period. Shweta's life had undergone a complete change within three weeks. She needed time to settle down and feel comfortable in her new home and among new people. But Vikrant was all too eager to consummate his marriage; after all, it was his legal right. Even with a good education and an American job, Vikrant had not been able to overcome his typical Indian patriarchal mindset. Thus, the hurried attempt at sex before he left for America left Vikrant dissatisfied and Shweta embarrassed.

When Shweta joined Vikrant in America, things improved for the couple. To Vikrant's credit, he did try to make life comfortable for Shweta. Shweta also tried to adjust to the new way of life. Tasks like shopping and setting up their home did help a friendship grow between them. But Vikrant and Shweta were two very different and distinct personalities. Vikrant was more of an outgoing person, while Shweta was someone who kept to herself. Vikrant enjoyed the company of friends, whereas Shweta would rather be surrounded by books. While Shweta took life seriously, Vikrant was hardly serious about anything. Shweta had expected Vikrant to help her with household chores and discuss his office-related activities with her, but Vikrant's patriarchal mindset hardly allowed him to do that. Good education and an American job had not helped Vikrant overcome his Indian patriarchal attitude. Perhaps Vikrant had wanted a wife who would dance to his tunes, and Shweta was fiercely independent with a mind of her own.

When the match between Vikrant and Shweta was fixed, the factors that were considered were the kind one usually finds in bio-data. But marriage is not employment, a job, or a service. It's a relationship meant to last a lifetime. Ideally, Vikrant and Shweta would have known each other quite well before tying the knot. They would have understood each other's likes, dislikes, habits, views, opinions, attitude, and outlook towards life. Then, they would have been in a better position to decide if they could spend the rest of their lives with each other. Here, they were thrust into marriage first, and then they were supposed to discover each other as a person. This arrangement was fraught with great risk; the risk of the unknown; of discovering some unpleasant fact about your spouse, hitherto unknown.

Now, let us consider the Jane factor. Because it was an arranged marriage, nobody knew about Jane. Had

Shweta known about Jane, she would, in all probability, not have married Vikrant. Hold on; it is not being suggested, even for a moment, that Jane was the cause of the breakdown of the marriage between Vikrant and Shweta. To Vikrant's credit, he had closed the Jane chapter and decided to start a new chapter with Shweta in his book of life. But Vikrant and Shweta were not on the same page when it came to most things in life. It was not that, because of Jane, Vikrant broke up with Shweta. On the contrary, it was because of the strife in their marriage that Vikrant drifted back towards Jane. Just consider this irony; although Vikrant had been in a relationship with Jane, knew her well, and was comfortable with her, he could not marry her, and he was married to Shweta, even when he did not know her fully well and was yet to reach a level of comfort with her.

Thus, as can be seen, the alliance between Vikrant and Shweta was brought about only because their academic qualifications, family background, and status were commensurate with each other. That they belonged to the same caste/community, and their horoscopes matched, were added attractions The issue of compatibility was never considered. It could not have been considered because Vikrant and Shweta neither knew each other nor loved each other. It was like they had to marry somebody, so why not marry each other? They hoped that they would get to know each other better after marriage, and eventually fall in love with each other. But it was only a hope. There is a huge difference between hope and a gamble. In this case, Vikrant and Shweta had played a gamble and hoped that it would pay off. But the stakes here were huge. Their entire future lives were at stake. And it all hung on hope and, probably, a prayer. Unfortunately, for Vikrant and Shweta, it was their compatibility, or rather the lack of it, that proved to be their undoing.

VII

ARRANGED MARRIAGE V/S LOVE MARRIAGE

This debate has been raging for ages. Advocates on either side drum up statistics to support their respective causes. However, statistics can often be misleading; they may not reveal the true picture. Firstly, in an institution like marriage, there cannot be a record of successful marriages, inasmuch as all marriages are performed with the intention of being successful. Nobody enters matrimony with the desire for their marriage to fail. So, the statistics can only be with respect to failed marriages, or in other words, marriages that ended in divorce. But here again, there's a catch. Not all unsuccessful marriages end in divorce. There have been cases where couples continue to put up with unhappy marriages for years for various reasons like societal disapproval, the future of children, or fear of an uncertain future. For wives, financial security could be an important reason for not wanting to rock the boat. Thus, statistics regarding divorce rates may not give an accurate picture of the success rate of marriages.

Traditionally, in India, people were averse to going in for a divorce. Indian society did not encourage divorce, and divorcees were looked down upon as if they had committed a sin. Indian society, as it is, is more concerned about customs and traditions rather than individual happiness. As such, bowing to societal pressure, Indian couples often continue with their unhappy marriages. Such couples simply exist; they do not live their lives.

The rates of divorce in India are the lowest in comparison to other countries. 1 out of every 100 marriages ends in a divorce in India. The rate is almost half that in the United States of America. However, in urban areas, the rates of divorce are getting higher over time. The rate of divorce has doubled since 1990 in cities like Mumbai and Delhi. Statistics show that 85% of divorces took place in the first three years of marriage. Now, what could be the reasons for the rise in divorce rates in India?

Some of the reasons for the rise in divorce rates in India are as follows:

1. Greater acceptance of divorce in society – No society is static. Social norms are always subject to external influences. Every society evolves over a period of time. Globalisation and economic liberalisation have not only influenced India's economy, but also its social mores. What was looked down upon yesterday has become

acceptable today, though not necessarily encouraged today. People's outlook towards divorce has changed. People have understood that an individual's happiness matters. This has led to a greater acceptance of divorce in Indian society.

2. Big cities and metros give the advantage of anonymity – Big cities like Mumbai and Delhi follow a certain work culture; they are driven by professionalism. People in such cities are more interested in getting their work done rather than being inquisitive about the personal lives of others. The sheer numbers in metros afford one anonymity, and professionalism helps to mask one's personal troubles. In villages and small towns, on the other hand, people not only have the time but also the inclination to poke their noses into the personal lives of others; besides, people often know each other in very small towns and villages. So urbanisation is one factor that has led to a rise in divorce rates in India.

3. Casual approach towards marriage – For today's generation, marriage is no longer sacrosanct. Even live-in relationships are not only seeing a rise but also acceptance in India. With the focus shifting to individualism, institutions like marriage are facing a challenge like never before.

The 'I-me-my' generation would not think twice before ending a marriage if they believe that they are not getting individual satisfaction out of the relationship, making compromises or sacrifices be damned.

4. DINKS Syndrome – Today, both husband and wife are well educated and carry highly paid jobs. Both are career-oriented and want to climb up the corporate ladder. They make a conscious decision not to have children. This has given rise to what are known as DINKS (Double Income, No Kids) couples. With no worries about kids and no issues about custody of children, divorce becomes a smooth affair. As it is, such couples are fiercely independent and competitive. The slightest issues or clash of egos, and they don't think twice before approaching a divorce lawyer.

5. Stress, lack of time for life partner – Life in big cities and metros like Mumbai and Delhi is highly stressful. Commuting woes, deadlines to be achieved, targets to be reached, corporate politics, rising inflation, and increasing demands all lead to stress. Working overtime, followed by long commutes, leaves hardly any time for life partners. Stress, coupled with a lack of time for a life partner, results in a compromised quality of marital relationships. Unless the couple makes conscious efforts to save their

relationship from deteriorating further, they end up in matrimonial courts.

6. Financial independence of women - Earlier, the role of women was largely confined to performing household chores. They were completely dependent on their husbands financially. And that made them vulnerable to abuse. Fear of losing financial security was the main reason why many women continued to suffer abuse, physical as well as mental, at the hands of their husbands. Today, an increasingly large number of women are gainfully employed. Financial independence and security have given women the means to stand up to and fight against abusive husbands. A financially independent woman would not continue to put up with an abusive husband but would walk out of the relationship, upholding her dignity and self-esteem.

So, these are some of the reasons for the rise in divorce rates in India. Although there has been a rise in the divorce rates, the divorce rate in India continues to be a lowly 1.1%. Does this indicate that a majority of Indians are happily married, or do many of them continue to suffer through unhappy marriages out of societal pressure? That is difficult to tell. Getting accurate data about a subject that is, by its nature, very personal is difficult.

As can be seen, the only data available is about the divorce rates in India, in general. There is no further bifurcation between divorce rates in arranged marriages and love marriages. This is because the data on divorce rates is probably secured from the matrimonial courts in India. The matrimonial courts are not going to maintain any record of how many arranged marriages and/or love marriages ended in a decree of divorce. It is not the job of a matrimonial court. Its job is only to maintain a record of the total number of cases filed and the total number of cases disposed of, either by decree of divorce or otherwise. So, that can only provide us with the rates of divorce in India, in general. Therefore, the statistics available neither help the advocates of arranged marriages nor those of love marriages.

However, there is some data available, though minuscule, which may help throw some light on the continuing debate. Now, consider this: according to UNICEF, the global divorce rate for arranged marriages is 6%. As per a recent survey by NDTV, 74% of Indians still prefer arranged marriages. This is bound to bring the smile back onto the faces of the advocates of arranged marriages. But, before the supporters of arranged marriages rush to proclaim victory, there are certain riders to be considered.

Insofar as the data provided by UNICEF, the global divorce rate for arranged marriages is 6%, which may appear to be on the lesser side, but it may not provide the complete picture. By its nature, an arranged marriage is not a relationship that binds two individuals but one that binds two families. In arranged marriages, the bond not only engages the husband and wife but also their respective families. Family members on either side get interwoven in the marital bond between the husband and wife. As such, an arranged marriage creates a social image for families on either side.

Therefore, if subsequently, an arranged marriage runs into trouble, it can lead to social consequences for families of both the husband and the wife. Since other family members are likely to be affected, the husband and wife in an arranged marriage may decide to continue living an unhappy married life rather than take the bold decision to separate. In arranged marriages, the weight of social pressure ensures that divorces hardly ever happen. On the contrary, in love marriages, it is the boy and the girl who themselves decide to enter into matrimony. In love marriages, the marital bond between the husband and wife may not necessarily involve or interweave their respective families. Since the decision to marry that particular boy or girl is taken by the individuals themselves, if any marital discord takes place in the future, the husband and wife are at liberty to reverse their decision. Since the decision to marry was their individual decision, they are not answerable to anybody and feel free to decide to go in for a divorce. Due to the lack of social pressure, couples in love marriages may not continue with an unhappy marriage. Thus, as can be seen, the rate of divorce by itself may not give a clear indication of the success of an arranged marriage. A true indicator of a successful marriage is the happiness quotient; the longevity of a marriage is no proof of its success, for success lies in happiness, not longevity.

Now, coming to the result of the survey by NDTV, viz., 74% of Indians still prefer arranged marriages. Does this sound like the victory bugle for arranged marriages? Well, not quite. India is a very vast and diverse country. It can be classified as urban vs. rural, metropolitan cities vs. tier-II & tier-III cities, educated vs. the not-so-educated, upper classes vs. the lower classes, one region or state vs. another region or state. Based on this classification, the results of the survey would vary. So, if love marriages are widely accepted in metropolitan cities, they may not be in small towns. Again, love marriages may have gained greater acceptance amongst the educated as compared to the not-so-educated. Further, certain regions and states in India still believe in *khaps*, *gotras*, and honour killings, which may be beyond the comprehension of people from other regions and states. Therefore, for the purpose of marital preference, to consider Indians as a whole, without taking into consideration the aforementioned disparities, would give a result that is not only skewed but oversimplified.

Even today, in India, parental pressure and parental choice play a huge role in marriages. The bride and the groom are selected as per their parents' choice, rather than the choice of the bride and the groom. If the boy and girl themselves decided to select their life partner, it would not only be unacceptable to their parents, but they would also be labelled as rebellious. If a boy and a girl are 'caught' seeing each other or courting each other, they would be labelled as being devoid of character. In such circumstances, how many young boys and girls would be ready to speak their minds and come out into the open in support of love marriages at the risk of inviting their parents' ire?

In this scenario, if a majority of Indians still prefer arranged marriages, it may not be an informed decision but rather dictated by parental pressure and social diktats. In fact, it would not be wrong to say that arranged marriages often take the form of forced marriages. But, the colour of customs and tradition helps camouflage the element of force involved in such marriages. The tearful scenes that are regularly played out at the '*bidaai*' of the bride are evidence enough of the involuntary force involved in the making of arranged marriages.

So, as far as the available data is concerned, it does not lead to any definite conclusion with regard to the success of arranged marriages, as against that of love marriages. Thus, the debate between arranged marriage and love marriage, on the point of success rate, remains inconclusive.

Since statistics have failed to help conclude the debate between arranged marriage and love marriage, does it mean that the status quo prevalent vis-à-vis arranged marriages should be allowed to continue? Are we not to question why? No one can predict the future of any relationship, more so a matrimonial one. Getting into a marital relationship is a gamble. Marriage is akin to playing flush, but while love marriage is comparable to playing flush after knowing your cards in hand, arranged marriage is playing blind flush. It doesn't require a genius to understand which one is fraught with more risks.

Now, just because statistics have not helped us conclude the debate between arranged marriage and love marriage does not mean that we accept and continue to follow an inherently flawed system in the name of custom and tradition. Societies evolve through a questioning and reasoning mind. Every relationship is built around certain core factors. Every marital relationship revolves around certain core factors, and the presence or absence of these factors, in varying degrees, would decide the success or otherwise of the marital relationship. Now, let us identify and consider what these core factors are, for these very factors will help us conclude the debate between arranged marriage and love marriage.

1. **Friendship:** "Marriage without friendship is like a bird without wings" – D. Schact. Friendship is the basic ingredient of every human relationship in this world. Whether it's neighbours, colleagues, friends, mates, parents, siblings, or spouses, it is the bond of friendship that helps the relationship to grow stronger. In marriage, the importance of friendship can't be over-emphasised; friendship is the foundation on which the entire relationship between a husband and wife stands. Just as for a high-rise building, its foundation has to be strong and solid, so also, for a marriage to be successful, the friendship between the spouses has to be strong and solid.

   The Oxford English Dictionary defines a "friend" as a person that one likes and knows well. That means, for someone to be your friend, you not only have to like that person but also know him or her well. Now, first of all, to like a person you have to know him or her well. Obviously, you cannot like a person unless you know him or her well.

   Firstly, how do you get to know a person well? You meet people in different settings, e.g., your neighbourhood, your college, your office, or even during your daily commute. As you meet the person often, you begin to know him or her better. As you get well acquainted with that person, you start meeting up with him or her, initially for a cup of coffee, then maybe for lunch, and finally for a movie. Gradually, from being just an acquaintance, that person becomes your friend. Once that person becomes your friend, you start spending more time with him or her. You share your thoughts with him or her. You look forward to meeting him or her. You not only share your happiness but also reveal your sorrows to him or her. When you get a similar response from him or her, you get to know each other well. After spending a lot of time together, you get to know each other's likes, dislikes, habits, choices, preferences, tastes, views, opinions, ideals, and even idiosyncrasies.

Having become friends, you come to the second stage, viz. getting to like him or her. You may have a lot of friends, but you may not like all of them equally; you may like some of them more than others. The reasons could be many; maybe you get along better with some of them than others. In this way, you may get to form what is known as your core group of friends.

Now, from this core group of friends, you may grow close to a particular friend belonging to the opposite sex. The two of you will, over a period of time, come to be known as what is called 'good friends'. It is, of course, not necessary that to discover a 'good friend' you need to have a core group of friends. You can get a 'good friend' even otherwise. So, a 'good friend' is one whom you not only know very well but also one whom you like more than the others. For our purpose, we are only restricting ourselves to a 'good friend' belonging to the opposite sex.

Over a period of time, you realise that your 'good friend' is not just that but 'something more than just a good friend'. It dawns upon you that maybe he or she is the life partner you were looking for. You begin to miss him or her if you don't meet him or her. You like talking to him or her, spending time with him or her, just being with him or her. You feel that your life is incomplete without him or her. You can't imagine your life without him or her. You don't want to lose him or her for anything in life. That's when you realise that your friendship has blossomed into love. The logical and natural end of this relationship is marriage.

So, how does friendship make love marriage superior to an arranged marriage? Well, as seen above, to begin with, spouses in a love marriage are good friends. They know each other very well, and having known each other very well, have begun to like each other, and having discovered love with each other, have decided to tie the knot. The friendship in a love marriage makes the spouses open, comfortable, and at ease with each other. They know exactly what to expect from their spouse, as well as what is expected of them. It is their friendship that has brought the spouses together in a love marriage.

On the contrary, in an arranged marriage, friendship is conspicuous by its absence. Amazingly enough, in arranged marriages, people often get married to total strangers. Now, applying the definition of "friend" to an arranged marriage scenario, it becomes obviously clear that the prospective bride and groom don't know each other well. They only have peripheral knowledge about each other, not personal knowledge. The knowledge that the prospective bride and groom have of each other is what is available in the public domain. So, when they don't even know each other well, the question of liking each other itself does not arise. In an arranged marriage, when a marriage proposal is accepted, what the prospective bride and groom like about each other are their respective appearances, education, occupation, family background, and social status. But what about liking each other as a person? Well, they cannot like each other because they hardly know each other.

In love marriages, there are no unpleasant surprises. The spouses not only know each other very well but have accepted each other after knowing each other's qualities. It can be said that, in a love marriage, there is an informed acceptance. In arranged marriages, on the other hand, spouses can be in for rude surprises. For instance, a husband who enjoys non-vegetarian food may discover after marriage that his wife is predominantly vegetarian, or a wife who hates smokers may discover, to her horror, after marriage, that her husband is a smoker. In love marriages, because the spouses are good friends, there is hardly anything that can be hidden from each other. Whereas, the whole idea in an arranged marriage is to impress the other side, so unpleasant information is often hidden until the marriage takes place. It is only after the marriage that the spouses discover unpleasant facts about each other, to their chagrin.

Another instance where love marriage scores over arranged marriage is in respect of the '*bidaai*' ceremony. In love marriages, because the bride and the groom are close friends since prior to their marriage, the girl often visits the boy's home. She not only gets well acquainted with his family members but also with his household. Over a period of time, as their friendship gets converted into courtship, the girl not only gets familiarised with the boy's household but begins to see it as her own home. So, during the *'bidaai'* ceremony, the bride goes laughing all the way to the groom's house. In arranged marriages, the *'bidaai'* is an emotional tear-jerker. Due to the lack of friendship between the bride and the groom, the bride sees herself going to reside in a strange place amongst stranger people. The thought of severing ties with the bride's parental home is so strong that often the emotional scenes witnessed at *'bidaai'* make it appear to be a funeral rather than a wedding.

Then again, in many arranged marriages, the wife doesn't address her husband by his name. She uses a sobriquet like *'Oji'* or *'Aho'*. She, therefore, calls to her husband as, *"Oji!! Sunte ho?"* After the birth of the first child, the husband would then be known by the name of the first child, e.g. *"Rahul ke papa"* or *"Seema ke daddy"*. If the wife is not even going to address the husband by his name, how is friendship expected to develop between them? The first sign of friendship between spouses is when the wife addresses the husband by his name. It creates a level playing field between them. It is a sign of gender equality. By using sobriquets like '*Oji*' or '*Aho*', the wife is always placing her husband on a pedestal, a false one at that. It is not required. The husband and wife are equal partners in their journey of life together, and that equality can only be brought about by friendship between them.

Ideally, friendship should form the underlying thread that runs in the relationship between a husband and wife. Friendship plays the role of glue that binds a husband and wife together. Friendship helps spouses to get rid of their inhibitions and feel comfortable in each other's company. Now, it can be argued that, even in an arranged marriage, friendship can develop between the spouses over a period of time. But, the point to be noted is that we make friends by choice and not by force. There cannot be forced friendship. Arranged marriages are all about forced friendships.

2. **Understanding:** Friendship is followed by understanding. In marriage, it is not enough for the spouses to simply know each other; they must understand each other. There is a subtle difference between 'knowing' and 'understanding'. To understand the difference between the two, let us consider a few examples: Many people have certain phobias; simply being aware that a certain person suffers from

a certain phobia is 'knowing', but being further aware of the causes and history as to why a certain person suffers from a certain phobia, and being able to appreciate it, is 'understanding'. Or, take another example; you may be aware that your friend holds very strong views about a particular subject. So much so that each time that subject is broached, he or she tends to get emotionally disturbed. That is 'knowing'. But when you know the reason behind your friend getting upset, you appreciate the situation in which your friend finds himself or herself, and you help him or her to cope with the situation, it is 'understanding'.

The Oxford English Dictionary defines "understanding" as sympathetic awareness or tolerance. To be sympathetically aware of others' feelings is to be understanding. Now, in love marriages, the couple not only knows each other very well but also understands each other. In fact, during the days of their courtship, it is this very understanding between them which prompts them to take the next step into matrimony. In arranged marriages, however, when the couple hardly know each other, to expect them to understand each other is expecting too much of them. In arranged marriages, the spouses are expected to get to understand each other after marriage. Excuse me, but life is no whodunit or a crime thriller where the mystery unravels in the end. What if the wife discovers after marriage that her husband is short-tempered and is unable to cope with his temper tantrums? What if the wife has a particular fetish, and the husband has no inkling about how to deal with it?

A marriage without understanding between the spouses is like a boat without oars; it will go nowhere. Understanding between a husband and wife adds a definitive meaning to their marital life. If there's no understanding between couples, there'll be a vacuum in their married life. Nothing can be riskier than to get married first, and then to expect the couple to get to understand each other. An arranged marriage is, however, fraught with this very risk.

3. **Trust:** If there is any one singular factor that can make or break a marriage, it is trust. In fact, every human relationship is built upon trust. A baby trusts its parents not to drop it while holding it; a child trusts its parents to take care of it and not to abandon it; a patient trusts his or her doctor to give the right treatment and cure his or her ailment; a businessman trusts another businessman not to be cheated in the business transaction; passengers trust pilots to fly them safely to their destination; all construction

work is based upon mutual trust amongst co-workers. An element of trust is involved in varying degrees in all our daily dealings with other human beings. Since marriage is the most intimate relationship that a human experiences in his or her life, the element of trust required in it is of the highest degree.

In certain cases, you have to trust another person even if you don't know that person too well. In most cases, this happens in the professional domain, where you trust the other person to perform his or her professional task well, although you may not know him or her personally, e.g., barber, plumber, electrician, driver, pilot, tailor, accountant, lawyer, doctor. But when it comes to personal relationships, trust is built slowly and gradually, as you get to know that person better over a period of time.

In personal relationships, therefore, trust is based on knowing the other person very well. As seen above, in the case of a love marriage, the spouses, prior to their marriage, are not only good friends but also know each other well and understand each other. Thus, this is a perfect setting for them, where they can learn to trust each other. In their case, trust precedes marriage. Because they trust each other, they decide to marry each other. As such, trust forms a strong pillar on which a love marriage stands.

In an arranged marriage, however, when the spouses don't even know each other well, the question of trusting each other would not arise. Yet, they are expected to trust each other. Why? Just because they happen to be lawfully married to each other? Does the legal marital bond itself ensure the trustworthiness of the partner? Lack of trust can create unnecessary strife in the relationship, e.g., the wife may accuse her husband of having extramarital affairs with his office colleagues, or the husband may become suspicious if he sees his wife talking to other men, including neighbours.

The relationship between a husband and wife has to grow with time, and for that, it has to be a healthy relationship. The relationship can be healthy if it is based on trust. A marital relationship based on mutual trust will be peaceful, happy, and fulfilling. Whereas a marital relationship based on mutual mistrust and suspicion will stutter and falter and ultimately end in divorce. In this context, how far does the system of arranged marriages, where trust is not gained but enforced, appear to be proper?

4. **Respect:** Respect for one another is the basic ingredient of all human relationships. Even a child needs to be respected. Needless to say, mutual respect between a husband and wife is a key factor for the success of their marital relationship.

   In a love marriage, the partners are already good friends, know each other well, understand each other, and also trust each other. This, in itself, leads them to respect each other.

   In an arranged marriage, on the other hand, the driving force is provided by customs and traditions. Traditionally, in Indian arranged marriages, the '*ladkewales*' are very demanding, and the '*ladkiwales*' have to cater to all their demands and fulfil their wishes. Also, all respect is reserved only for the '*ladkewales*'. After marriage, the wife has to respect not only her husband but also her in-laws and a host of other relatives. Every wish of the husband and other elders in the family has to be fulfilled the moment it is expressed. The status of a newly married wife is more of a maid rather than the daughter-in-law of the house. Sometimes, she is also kept away from the discussions involving financial matters of the household. The newly married wife is made to feel like an outsider. While the wife has to respect each and every member of the husband's family, scant respect is shown to the newly married wife. In the case of a love marriage, the husband would stand up for his wife, but in an arranged marriage, the husband would only play the role of an onlooker, bound as he is by customs and traditions. The patriarchal system, where women have to cover their heads and faces before family elders, are not allowed to voice their opinions, and their role is confined to managing household chores, is not only disrespectful of women but also downright opposed to gender equality.

When you respect your wife, you respect womanhood. In households where wives are respected by their husbands, children, especially sons, grow up learning to respect women. Most offences against women take place because men, as sons, are not taught to respect women at home.

In a love marriage, mutual respect between spouses ensures gender equality. In arranged marriages, it is the wife who is called upon to respect her husband — not because she finds him worthy of respect but only because he happens to be her husband — whereas, no such counter obligation is placed upon the husband. Equilibrium between spouses ensures stability in marriage. Any marriage where one party is treated less equal than the other is bound to be an unhappy one.

5. **Love:** "Why do you want to marry?" The only apt answer to this question would be, "For love."

   Ever wondered why men work so hard to provide their wives and children with the best that life has to offer? Why do women strive so hard to provide the best care for their families? Why do children strive so hard to achieve success that will make their parents proud? The only emotion that drives these men, women, and children is love. Yes, it is love that makes the world go round. It is love that makes everybody return home at the end of the day. In today's material world, it would appear as if everybody is hankering for money. Maybe so, but that money is required for love. It is required to provide a better life to loved ones. Take away love, and what use would that money be? It is love that adds meaning to life and makes it worth living.

   Love is of great significance in marriage. It is the singular most important reason why one marries. Love is the fodder that sustains marriage. There are ups and downs in life; there could be financial setbacks or a health condition; if there is love, one can get through the most difficult problems in life. It is love for which people work, earn, spend, laugh, enjoy, cry, feel hurt, live for, and die for. There can be love without marriage, but there cannot be marriage without love. It can be said that love is the oxygen that breathes life into a marriage.

Now, coming to a love marriage, the partners are good friends, know each other very well, understand each other, trust each other fully, and respect each other. At this stage, they realise that they are more than just 'good friends'. It dawns upon them that they are actually in love with each other. Marriage comes as a natural progression, to formalise their relationship. After being in love for some time, it is the desire to settle down in life with the person whom you love the most that leads to the couple deciding to tie the knot. Thus, in a love marriage, love precedes marriage. In other words, in a love marriage, the couple gets married because they love each other.

Now, let's consider the case of an arranged marriage. Here, the bride and the groom hardly know each other, so the question of understanding each other and trusting each other does not arise. The bride may respect the groom more out of social pressure than because she finds him worthy of respect. Obviously, when the bride and the groom don't even know each other well, they cannot be expected to be good friends. Without any semblance of friendship between the bride and the groom, obviously they can't be expected to be in love with each other. If not for love, then why are they getting married? Well, because their parents think they would make a good couple. In other words, their parents expect them not only to become good friends after marriage but also to love each other after marriage. Haven't we heard of the phrase, "To fall in love..."? Love is a spontaneous emotion; love just happens. Love cannot be forced upon anybody. You cannot force anybody to love you. By getting the young couple to marry each other and then expecting them to start loving each other, only because they are married to each other, is to present them with a fait accompli. What if, in a given instance, the couple doesn't begin to love each other after marriage, for whatever reason? Are they then supposed to live through a loveless marriage? Or are they supposed to have extramarital affairs? All parents who push their children into arranged marriages are required to answer these questions. And please, no clichéd replies like, "In India, it happens like this only." Should youngsters in India not have the freedom to choose their own life partner? After all, they have to spend their entire life with that person.

Why should they be forced to marry someone of their parents' choice, and then force themselves to love that person? Is love that inconsequential in marriage that two strangers can comfortably get married to each other only because the elders in their family feel that they would make a good husband and wife pair? And, all those who harbour false pretensions about Indian culture and claim that all arranged marriages finally end in the couple getting to love each other, that is not love. Being presented with a fait accompli, it can, at the most, be called a settlement or even a compromise, but definitely not love. There can never be love without spontaneity. So also, there can never be marriage without love.

Now, let us consider the nomenclature used to describe the two types of marriages. In cases of the former, as the name suggests, love is an integral part of the marriage. It is clear from the name itself that love is the reason for the marriage taking place. However, in the case of the latter, the word 'love' is conspicuous by its absence.

The word 'arranged' gives a meaning of it being a planned and formal event. Without 'love', the feeling of spontaneity, passion, and longing go missing in an 'arranged' marriage. The words 'love marriage' itself create an image of a much-in-love couple getting married for their own sake. Whereas the words 'arranged marriage' conjure up the image of a couple formally selected to marry each other for the sake of others. Why has the word 'love' been deliberately kept out of the nomenclature 'arranged marriage'?

6. **Sex:** This is one factor which is the least discussed when it comes to marriage, yet it is one of the crucial factors for a happy married life. In India, talking about sex is taboo. Even while discussing marriage, sex is avoided. People behave as if it is non-existent. Yet, India continues to be the second most populous country in the world, next only to China. If everybody is doing it, why shy away from admitting it?

   When it comes to sex, Indians, as a people, are a repressed lot. In India, expressing one's sexuality is often misunderstood as being promiscuous. Being open-minded about one's sexuality is attributed to harmful Western influences and is denounced as being opposed to Indian culture and values. For the kind information of these Indian culture-vultures, '*Kama Sutra*' was product of India. Also, the highly acclaimed sculptures of Khajuraho are evidence enough that people in ancient

India were very much evolved when it came to sexuality. It was the British who imposed Victorian puritanical values on Indians because they wanted to subject the entire sub-continent to their administrative control. As things stand today, Britain has long ago gotten rid of the Victorian prudish values, whilst we in India continue to cling to them in the mistaken belief that they represent Indian culture and values.

Why is sex looked upon as a shameful act? Is it not a biological need of the body? If there's nothing wrong in quenching one's thirst or satisfying one's hunger, why is satisfying one's sexual desire considered undesirable or even shameful? Of course, the reference to sex here is only to consensual sex. Any sexual act which is not consensual amounts to a sexual offence and deserves the harshest punishment under the law. But, when consensual sex is suppressed, under the mistaken belief that it is against Indian culture and values, it not only leads to personality disorders but also creates social tension. People are happy when they are neither thirsty, hungry, nor sexually starved. It is scientifically proven that hugging your loved ones releases feel-good hormones in the body. But, the kind of moral policing that goes on in India does not even allow couples to hold hands in public. Since the idea of privacy is anathema to most Indians, even married couples have to devise ingenious ways and means to snatch some private moments.

What is the importance of sex in marriage? A Vedic sage emphasised that the basis of a happy and fulfilling married life is the sense of unity, intimacy, and love between husband and wife physically, mentally, and spiritually. Hence, a wife is considered to be the '*Ardhangini*' of her husband as per Hindu tradition. Thus, the role of sex in marriage is not only restricted to procreation. Marriage not only brings about an emotional union between husband and wife but also brings about a physically intimate union. Marriage is not only about a meeting of minds between the spouses but also a meeting of bodies between them. The union between a husband and wife is complete in all respects when their marriage is consummated. That's why any problem or irritant that interferes with the sexual cohesion between spouses can lead to disastrous results, including divorce.

Now, in love marriages, the partners are not only good friends but are also in love with each other. Being in love, they are very comfortable in each other's company; they have no inhibitions. In love marriages, the partners are already united emotionally; so physical union comes as a natural progression in their relationship. In a love marriage, sex is the culmination of a beautiful romantic relationship. It comes more as an expression of complete love rather than as lust. In certain cases, the partners may have also indulged in pre-marital sex during their period of courtship. Nothing objectionable in that, as long as it is consensual sex between two responsible adults. If anything, it only helps the couple to understand each other better and sort out any problems that they may face in future in discharging their sexual functions in marriage. In that way, a live-in relationship serves as a trial-and-error method. Better to take a trial to see if the two can live as husband and wife on a long-term basis rather than to jump into matrimony and later end up with a messy divorce.

In arranged marriages, on the other hand, the partners are neither good friends nor in love with each other. Actually, they don't even know each other well. In such circumstances, sex becomes an uncomfortable prospect. In an arranged marriage, when the bride leaves her parental home and goes to reside in her matrimonial home with the groom, she is already emotionally disturbed. She has to adjust in a new home with new people whom she doesn't know too well. At that time, sex is the last thing on her mind. The husband, however, is all too eager to consummate the marriage at the earliest. Having got married, the husband considers it his right, both legal and moral, to get physically intimate with his newly married wife. The husband's desire almost borders on lust. The wife finds herself in an awkward situation. At that stage, it is akin to making love with a stranger, and yet she is bound, both legally and morally, to do it as a dutiful wife. Sex is more of a mental act, although it is executed physically. If there is even a slight element of involuntariness in the sexual act, it can have disastrous consequences. Any couple which begins its marital life with episodes of failed or unsatisfactory sexual encounters is looking at an unhappy future. An unsatisfactory sexual relationship can mar an otherwise satisfactory marriage. Sexual problems in such arranged marriages can finally lead to divorce. And the only reason for this is that the couple is forced into a sexual relationship by an arranged marriage. Just as love is a spontaneous emotion sex, too, should happen on its own; it cannot be forced upon. In a worst-case scenario, forced sex in marriage can also enter the realm of marital rape.

7. **Compatibility:** This is the x-factor in a marriage. This factor singularly decides the success, or otherwise, of the marriage in the long run.

   The Oxford English Dictionary defines "compatible" as "(of two people) able to have a good relationship; well-suited." We make friendships only with those people who are like-minded and with whom we share similar thoughts and interests. Two or more persons share a harmonious relationship when their views are well-matched. What holds true for friendship also holds true for marriage. After all, marriage is based on friendship between the spouses. For a husband and wife to be compatible with each other, they have to be well-suited. Now, to qualify as being well-suited, their characteristics have to match with each other. Primarily, characteristics can be classified into two types: acquired and innate. Acquired characteristics include educational qualifications, employment opportunities, economic status, and social standing. Innate characteristics would include physical appearance, habits, behaviour, likes and dislikes, views and opinions, tastes, and passions.

   Let us now take the case of a love marriage. In a love marriage, the partners are very good friends and know each other very well.

They know each other's characteristics, both acquired and innate, very well, and either because of or in spite of these characteristics, they fall in love with each other. At this stage, the couple shares a good relationship with each other. As far as the compatibility factor is concerned, in a love marriage, the couple is tested before the marriage itself. So, the outlook for a love marriage, on the touchstone of compatibility, is very positive. In case it is not positive or is even negative, the couple can call off their relationship before getting into matrimony and save themselves from messy divorce proceedings later on.

Now, let us consider the case of an arranged marriage. In an arranged marriage, the spouses are only aware of the acquired characteristics of each other. At the time of their marriage, the spouses are not aware of the innate characteristics because, at that stage, they are neither good friends nor do they know each other too well. Just because a particular person has attractive acquired characteristics is no guarantee that he or she also has good innate characteristics. A man may hold good academic qualifications, but he may be badly behaved and abusive. Similarly, a woman may be successfully employed, but she may be found wanting in manners and etiquettes. The success of marriage does not depend merely on acquired characteristics. On the contrary, marriage, being a very personal and intimate relationship, often depends on good innate characteristics being possessed by the spouses. Good acquired characteristics are of no use because experience shows that it is the lack of good innate characteristics that often leads to disagreements and discontent in a marriage. Thus, in an arranged marriage, the compatibility of the couple is never tested before the marriage. The couple is considered suitable for each other only on the basis of their acquired characteristics. It is only after the marriage that the couple realises that they are unable to have a good and harmonious relationship because their innate characteristics are not well-matched. In an arranged marriage, it is only post-marriage that the couple discovers that they are not compatible with each other.

As can be seen, the core factors around which every marriage revolves are friendship, understanding, trust, respect, love, sex, and compatibility. The success, or otherwise, of a marriage depends on how well these factors are received in the marital relationship. As seen earlier, these core factors manifest positively in the case of love marriages. It can be said that, in love marriages, to begin with, these core factors are present in abundant measure. Love marriages, therefore, begin on a positive note, with high energy levels. In the case of arranged marriages, however, to begin with, these core factors are more or less absent. Arranged marriages, therefore, begin differently. There is a lot of suspense in arranged marriages. As there is uncertainty in arranged marriages, it leads to anxiety amongst the spouses. In arranged marriages, it is left to the spouses to discover each other after marriage. To the couple's good fortune, if the discovery is a happy one, all goes well for them. Unfortunately for them, if the discovery is not what they had expected, they become the subject of sympathy. Both the husband and wife accuse each other of having tricked them into marriage. Thus, an arranged marriage is very high on expectation about the spouses, but very low on knowledge about each other. It would not be incorrect to say that destiny decides the fate of arranged marriages. On the other hand, in love marriages, the couple charts their own destiny.

Advocates of arranged marriages can be seen up on their feet, scrambling to support the age-old system. They would vociferously argue that not all love marriages are successful and not all arranged marriages end up as failures. Yes, agreed. It is a correct observation being made, but let us analyse the reasons behind it.

Firstly, all humans are complex beings. As such, every human relationship is complicated. A marital relationship, being highly personal and intimate, is probably the most complicated of all human relationships. It is, therefore, almost impossible to predict, with reasonable accuracy, the future of such a complex human relationship. Secondly, in the long run, there can be a drastic change in the circumstances, different from those prevailing at the time of marriage. Different people react to changes in circumstances in different ways. The outlook of people, over a period of time, does change with changes in age, time, and circumstances. Thus, a husband and wife in their fifties would react to a particular circumstance differently than they would have in their twenties. The physical ability and mental patience of every individual to handle a particular situation undergo a complete change with changes in age, time, and circumstances. All marriages, whether love or arranged, are subject to changes in circumstances over a period of time. How the spouses adapt themselves to these changes determines the success of their marriage.

Thirdly, in love marriages, it is solely the decision of the spouses themselves to marry each other. So, if they discover, after marriage, that they have made a wrong decision, they do not hesitate to correct their mistake. After all, they have only themselves to blame for having made a wrong choice. In arranged marriages, however, the decision to marry is a family decision, often taken by family elders. So, issues like family honour and societal pressure often deter spouses from taking any drastic steps, and they continue with their unhappy marriages.

It has never been suggested during the course of the debate that all love marriages are successful or that all arranged marriages are doomed to fail. Only a naive person would dare to make such a suggestion. The entire purpose behind the discussion was to understand and appreciate why love marriages, as an institution, are considered better than arranged marriages. We have seen how the core factors of friendship, understanding, trust, respect, love, sex, and compatibility manifest themselves positively in the case of love marriages. We have also seen how, to begin with, these core factors are missing in the case of arranged marriages. We have also noted that available statistics on divorce do not help to advance our debate further. The whole idea behind the discussion was to find out which system of marriage appears to be better suited from the perspective of the newly married couple. The entire perspective of the discussion was only from the point of view of the newly married couple. It can be concluded, based on the discussion, that in a love marriage, the couple enters matrimony on a positive note, with high energy levels. In a love marriage, the couple is in familiar territory. On the other hand, in an arranged marriage, the couple treads cautiously and diffidently. In an arranged marriage, the couple is in strange and uncharted territory.

Now, the problem is that people, in general, and Indians, in particular, are subject to inertia. When it comes to social customs and traditions, Indians are loath to question them. What has been practised for ages is often unquestioningly accepted as correct. The human race is the most intelligent living race on Earth. No other creature on Earth has a brain as advanced as that of a human. The human brain has designed skyscrapers, bridges, tunnels, airplanes, rockets, submarines, computers, smartphones, and the internet. It has also made great strides in the field of medical science. Then, why does this intelligent human brain continue to accept age-old customs, traditions, and practices, even when they don't appear to be just, fair, reasonable, and correct? The human brain has the rare ability to reason. Why, then, is this faculty not used to question outdated systems, traditions, and institutions?

We have seen how the system of arranged marriages in India not only places the newly married couple in an uncomfortable position but, in fact, is akin to gambling with their future lives. It is time the intelligentsia in India take a good hard look at the prevailing customs, traditions, and practices and rid India of those that have lost their relevance or become inconsistent with the modern age. It is time we have a relook at the system of arranged marriages prevailing in India. It is time we stop being obsessed with the concept of 'marriageable age', so much so that, in our quest to get our children married at a marriageable age, we compromise and neglect the core factors that make up for a happy marital relationship. It is time we stop being obsessed with the concept of "being married" and concentrate on the concept of "being happy", whether married or otherwise. It is time we review the system of arranged marriages in India.

www.ingramcontent.com/pod-product-compliance
Lightning Source LLC
LaVergne TN
LVHW091100150826
845673LV00002B/664

* 9 7 9 8 8 9 4 4 6 3 2 9 2 *